DEKERS BLUE LINE CLUB

a full-length novel, written by

STEPHEN M. CONTI

PublishAmerica
Baltimore

First printing

ISBN: 1-4137-1197-9
PUBLISHED BY PUBLISHAMERICA, LLLP
www.publishamerica.com
Baltimore

Printed in the United States of America

TABLE OF CONTENTS

This book is dedicated to:

Kathryn E. Thomas,
who always convinced me that
what I did was great and forever
encouraged me to continue.

Thank you from the
bottom of my heart.

PROLOGUE
June 2001

Well, this was it. Four long, hard years of high school had rapidly come to a close. Four years of friendships, cliques and social gatherings. Four years of academics, with favorite teachers and those upon whom we wished death (jokingly, of course). Four years of team sports, pep rallies, state tournaments, championship trophies and the like. Four years of school dances, formal or casual, date or no date. Four years of love found, and often lost. Four years of Amy. Four great years.

Memories passed before my eyes, as I stood motionless, staring at the graduation setup, standing in the center of our school football field. The oversized 'Class Of 2001' banner hung above the stands, where my classmates and I would sit during the ceremony. Looking at the steadily increasing crowd, I spotted my parents and brother near the top of the steep stands as I flashed a wave in their direction. They, however, were looking elsewhere.

My watch read five-thirty in the p.m. as I opened the car door to my Honda Accord and grabbed two articles of clothing, neatly arranged on hangers. I sported a green collared shirt with brown khaki pants and began to fasten my Stafford tie around my neck. The gown was a light blue shade for the boys and white for the girls, our traditional school colors. The tassels on our caps were much the same, with white and blue strings and of course, the '01' in gold. Personally, if you ask me, it was quite the eyesore; at least the way it looked on a t-shirt and jeans guy like myself.

Footsteps approached my vehicle to the left as without looking up, I knew exactly who stood before me.

"Hey babe," I said to the shadow in the dirt.

"How did you know it was me?"

"Easy," I replied. "You're the only person that doesn't run up to me screaming and yelling about something ridiculous." I picked my head up to look at the lovely girl in white, flashing her shiny white teeth. "Plus, you have the cutest shadow I've ever seen."

Amy Lewis blushed uncontrollably. She was already dressed in her cap and gown and held her 'national honor society' sash in her left hand. "Are you ready for this?" asked my misty-eyed girlfriend.

"As ready as I'll ever be, I suppose. This came up too fast." I flashed a sudden smile at Amy. "Want to tie my tie?"

"Sure," she agreed. "You don't know how to tie your own neckties yet?"

"Oh, I do. This way will be quicker though, I can put my robe on at the same time."

"I think it's called a gown," corrected Amy while making a perfect knot.

"A gown just sounds weird for a guy to wear."

"Well, whatever it's called, you're putting it on backwards." I often *did* make a fool of myself. Sooner or later, you'll learn that about me.

Graduates began to file into Lannon Field, after most hugged relatives and went through separate entrances. With cap and gown on, I walked hand-in-hand with Amy underneath the stands. The 253 kids from the graduating class would set up here and promptly at six p.m. , would march directly onto the field, double file, to the traditional tune of Pomp & Circumstance. I anticipated cameras to be clicking wildly from the many *relieved* parents, especially mine.

I took my place in the alphabetical line right behind Tracey Calder and next to James Cotter, neither of which I spoke to in my four years. Amy stood about 90 people back with my other low-lettered friends. Buddies Matt, Kurt, Eric, Sara, Liz, Scotty and Oscar stood in the back third of the line, nearly out of sight. As I waited for the ceremony to get underway, a memory of the clan and I from sophomore year passed by. We had many of them, good and bad. Thinking about it all made me wonder if we'd all be together after graduation. I could use a few familiar faces when I departed for Ann Arbor in the fall.

The time was six and right on cue, the 50-piece concert band could be heard playing the introduction.

"Here we go."

Our high school teachers scrambled around, attempting to get us onto the field and into the stands in a somewhat orderly fashion.

"No talking everyone! Be sure to walk slow!"

I inched forward as the first lines of graduates promenaded out to the cheers of all the spectators. I must say, the air horns sounding took me a bit by surprise. It was like a goal being scored by the Red Wings.

As I got nearer to the double doors, held open by Mr. and Mrs. Wellington, the sun shone down into my eyes. It felt as if I was walking through the gates to the rest of my life.

The scene was one that all graduating seniors never forget. Sitting with your cap and gown, diploma in hand, next to the hundreds of others being let loose into the world and accepting congratulations from every high-up in town. It was a rare opportunity to be the center of attention.

"Welcome Fenton High Graduating Class of 2001!" I remember Mayor Southwick announcing in his annual opening speech. "And let me be the first to say, congratulations! It is with great honor that I speak here tonight at this commencement ceremony as I have done in years past. You, class of 2001, have made it!" Applause. "Soon, the world will look to all of you for leadership and assistance and every one of you will be well prepared to succeed in your various endeavors. Who knows what the future may bring. We may have our future president of the United States sitting among us tonight, or the next CEO of a major business corporation. Perhaps one of our graduates will set foot on the moon or be the first to discover a new planet in our solar system. The point I'm trying to make is that any one of you graduates can achieve the world. Make the best of your future and good luck to you all!"

The speech went something like that. Many others followed, including a message from the principal, a reading by Father Spiro and the lame valedictorian speech.

When it was finally time to receive our diplomas, my parents were positioned with camera at the ready.

"I'm nervous!" exclaimed Tracey, turning around to face me.

"You'll be fine, it'll be over before you know it."

"You think so?"

"Sure." I answered the short, brown-haired girl. "Just shake the guy's hand, pick up the diploma and head back for the stands."

"I know. I'm just afraid I'll trip or something."

As she spoke, class president Omar Rodriguez spoke clearly into the microphone, "Tracey M. Calder." The nervous girl strutted forward, all smiles, and completed the task without error.

"David E. Calvetto," stated my friend Omar as he glanced up from the roster and nodded at me.

A few air horns blew and cheering came from all over as my name was read. I gave a wave and a corny salute to the bleachers while walking up to the smiling principal.

"Congratulations Dave!"

"Thank you, sir."

Would life ever be the same after this moment? I had officially graduated from high school and although delighted, emotions ran wild. I would have three more summer months to spend in Fenton before the real journey began. Amy would go south to Bowling Green University while I, like most graduating seniors, would attend the pride of UM.

Sitting in the stands that night, I never knew anybody named Sean Collins, Jerry Trodeau, Derek Strickland or Scott Hooden. I hadn't met Tanya Aiken or Gerry Walsh or Alex Hutchinson or even Michael Stutzel. Sitting there that warm and humid evening, I never knew these people would forever be part of my life.

September 2002

1

It's an absolute sin to wake up before 10 o'clock on a Saturday morning. Seriously, the entire town of Ann Arbor, Michigan, doesn't open its doors until at least noon, giving the thousands of hung-over kids ample time to recuperate. At the hour I awoke, there were probably college kids still stumbling back to their dorms after a hard night of partying and they would then proceed to sleep the entire day long, something I could never understand. I, however, was in my bed at 11 the previous night, attempting to get a healthy seven hours of good sleep. I knew that I was going to need it.

As soon as my alarm clock beeped and flashed 6:15, nerves had paralyzed my body. They weren't nerves of terror, but rather butterflies of excitement, as I thought of the morning that lay before me. Well, maybe I was a little frightened, but mostly excited. Yeah, that sounds good. I was optimistic for the most part, knowing I had worked at this for the majority of my life—eleven years to be exact—and it's still hard to believe I began this when I was merely 8 years old, learning from my father almost every afternoon. Actually, on the subject of old memories, I recall my dad picking me up early for a doctor's appointment on many occasions. We always wanted to get some rink time in before the sun went down on cold winter nights. Sure, moms never knew any of this, but trust me, it was better that way. I enjoyed playing hockey and still do today, which allows the excitement to overpower the terrifying fright.

The coach wanted us all on the ice at 8 o'clock sharp, wearing equipment and fully prepared to work. I had laced up my skates and began to warm up half an hour early. Surprisingly, about ten freshman or potential first year players were already there, skating in circles, practicing their puck handling and firing slap shots into both vacant nets. The lights were dim inside the 7,000-seat Yost Ice Arena, giving it an eerie, early-morning feel. This feeling was all too common for me, as I had tried out for the hockey squad as a measly freshman, but got cut after only the first day. It was shocking to see the skill level of the other kids, all wanting to make the elusive spot on one of the top teams in the country, all willing to kick someone else's ass to get there.

This go around, I knew what to expect. Now, as a sophomore, I had a year of competitive college hockey under my belt, playing for a tough intramural league that exhibited a high skill level. Basically, everyone who got rejected from the big team skated in this club, which ran from early November to February. I was pretty beat up by the end of the season, but I knew the university's team played games from early October until April (if they were lucky enough to make the playoffs), so all summer, I worked on my endurance, which would help me during tryout week at least. I hit the gym on a normal basis and when I wasn't working my summer job, I'd be at the town's skating rink. Well, that's not EXACTLY true. I managed to spend a lot of time with my girlfriend, as we extended our relationship to two years in August. That's right, she's my high school sweetheart. It's a little more difficult now as she attends Bowling Green University in Ohio, which is nearly a two-hour drive from the campus of Michigan. However, it's no need to worry; we see each other nearly every weekend and I hate to get all mushy, but we love each other very much. This reminded me, I had to call Amy (my girlfriend if you didn't figure it out), right after practice to tell her either the good or bad news. Even if the news was good, I couldn't get too excited; there would still be three tryout days after this, leaving plenty of time to get screwed over.

The floodlights turned on inside the Yost Ice Arena. It was nearly blinding until my eyes could adjust to the brightness of the structure. It was 10 minutes to eight on that Saturday morning and I had begun my morning stretches, working primarily on my legs. As I laid flat on the ice with one leg pointed in the air, I noticed how the rink was much more crowded than it had been twenty minutes previous. I estimated approximately thirty nervous college kids (and those few cocky ones) preparing on the ice, maybe seven to ten more on the bench and around the boards, and twenty or so spectators who got lost in a sea of blue seats. I didn't particularly like people watching me try out, but I guess I'd have to get used to it if I made the team. The arena would be full and rocking, watching your every move.

I didn't recognize any of the other hockey players on the ice, probably because—I assumed—most of them were merely freshmen. Actually, I really didn't know too many people at UM—I'm a fairly shy person. Parties were not my thing as I always opted to go home on weekends and see my girlfriend. I never understood the big enjoyment in getting drunk anyway; it'll empty your wallet and make you sick at the same time. Amy enjoys drinking occasionally, which usually makes me a little nervous inside. I know how stupid people can be while intoxicated and how all brain cells have the tendency to disappear. But hey, even though I got a little uneasy, I trusted Amy very much and knew she'd never hook up with another guy, as the college lingo goes.

Eight o'clock. The coach and his crew wasted no time as they approached center ice and called for us to gather around. Dressed in a black polo shirt, wind pants, expensive black Bauer skates and a whistle hanging from his neck, world famous hockey coach, Jerry Trodeau scanned the faces of his potential players. He shook his head, whispered something to one of his colleagues, laughed out loud, and looked as if he was ready to speak. It was quite intimidating sitting in front of one of the top coach's in the nation.

"Good morning everyone," belted Jerry Trodeau, the voice of a true winning hockey skipper.

Silence. We really *were* quite nervous.

"Well, as you can all see, there are quite a few of you here. My list reads fifty-four trying out for the team, and it looks like we have at least that many today. Unfortunately, the NCAA limits collegiate hockey rosters to twenty-two, including the two reserves, and we already have fifteen players on the team. So, do the math boys. Only seven of you will be suiting up for the blue and yellow this year.

"Now, there will be four days of intense two to three hour practices: today, Monday, Tuesday and Thursday. We'll be cutting approximately twenty of you after today's skate and nine to ten on each remaining day. Don't take it personally, we'd like to have all of you on the team, but everyone that follows Michigan hockey knows we are a very competitive program. We only have room for the few of you that will make a big positive impact on our club, which is much harder than it sounds. It involves getting on the ice for a minimum of ten playing minutes a game and getting your ass kicked around. We don't have a problem with that. However, it's those of you who kick back that succeed at this game." The coach paused to clear his throat.

"I'd like to take a few seconds and introduce the coaching staff. From my left, our trainer, Ed Blackwell. Those of you who play for the yellow and blue will get to know Ed very well. Next to him is one of our assistant managers, Jeff Ridley. He's been involved with the hockey program for nine years now and enjoys acting as the team counselor." Jeff chuckled at this personal joke and waved his hand to the kids kneeling in front of him. "To his right is our second assistant manager, Red Blemenson and at the end, our bench manager, Richard Hunt." Both waved respectively. "Feel free to go to them with questions at any time.

"All right boys, it's time to show us what you've got. Let's have all prospective goalies go to the far corner of the ice, defensemen at the opposite corner, and centers and wingers, meet me down by the north goal. Good luck to everyone and I hope to see you on my team this year." Tweet!

Spoken like a true hockey coach. It was a little odd hearing the same speech two years in a row and I was hoping this would be the last time. Hoping. My heart basically sank when Coach Trodeau told us only seven players would make the squad out of 54, or probably even more. I figured that to be around 12 or 13 percent—extremely low from my vantage point. But, you know, take it one day at a time and all that stuff.

That's pretty much how I did it too. I literally skated and played my butt off that Saturday morning, horse-whipping my CCM's into action and actually receiving a few comments from Jerry Trodeau himself.

Well, all he really said was, "Nice shot number eight," after I netted one of my two goals in a scrimmage game. Coming from the two-time Coach of the Year, however, I was taken back by the comment, and to tell you the truth, honored.

It was eleven o'clock and I was pretty damn tired. Sitting on an uncomfortable wooden bench in the home team's locker room, I ran a hand through my thick blonde hair, removing some of the excess sweat. All my padding remained attached with the exception of my grungy white helmet, which sat beside me. Even the ratty old University of Michigan jersey that was distributed during practice remained over my chest protector. I wore the blue uniform with the faded yellow letters as a sign of pride for the team, and not to mention, I looked pretty good in it.

It was still a good hour before the coach and his mates would tack up the dreaded cut list. I figured this gave me time to change out of my smelly gear and grab an early lunch across the way at Zippy's, best known, and cheapest, fast food joint around the massive campus. From time to time, I'd skip dinner at the dining halls to order a toasted steak & cheese from Zippy's, mainly to avoid getting a stomachache for the night. There were always empty tables there and I figured I could relax before facing the moment of truth.

As I bent down to unlace my skates, a surprisingly firm hand was placed on my shoulder. The tap startled me as I jerked my head upwards to see none other than Jerry Trodeau!

"Hey, we'll see you Monday afternoon, yeah?" spoke the coach in his Canadian accent.

What?! Did he just tell me I made the cut? Does he know what position I played? Does he even know my name? Who cares!

"You bet! Thank you Coach Trodeau," I managed to spit out in the nerdiest of fashions.

He gave me a slight smile, shook his head, tucked his clipboard underneath his arm and walked away towards the vacant office at the end of the hall. The whole time, I just sat there and stared at him strolling away with that certain swagger of importance. I didn't even have to wait for the cut list! One of my idols personally invited me back for the second try-out! Man, I must have made such a great impression on....

"Hey, you alive?" came a deep voice from next to me.

"Whoa! Hey, sorry, I didn't even see you there."

"Yeah, I noticed. Congratulations on making it past today, you looked sharp out there."

"Thanks man," I replied to the abnormally muscular kid. I try to use 'man' whenever I can in a sentence; it gives me more of that college appearance.

"I'm Sean," the kid said while sticking his hand out. "Sean Collins."

"Nice to meet you, I'm Dave." I gladly accepted the friendly handshake and attempted to hide my shyness. Sean appeared to tower above me in height as he stood there with poise. He had to be at least 6 foot 2, which was enormous, compared to little 67 inch me. Sean had the build of a true hockey defenseman. With his bare chest showing, it looked as if he could drill me straight into the ground simply by popping me lightly on top of the head. His short black hair and goatee gave him a rough-looking exterior, but I could tell by the way this kid talked, he meant no harm to anyone.

"So are you a freshman too?" asked Sean. Too?! I would have taken him for at least 21 years old.

"No, no, I'm a sophomore. I gave it a shot last year, but got cut on the first day."

"Ah, sorry to hear that bro. At least you know what to expect this year though." That sounded familiar.

"Yeah, up until now anyway. I don't know shit from now on in." He chuckled at this remark. That's another rule of college; when you have the opportunity to swear, always utilize it.

"Well, good luck to you Dave. You're already one step ahead of me, I'm still sweatin' it out today!" exclaimed Sean Collins.

"Good luck to you too. I'll probably see you Monday."

"Let's hope."

What a great morning. I survived the first hockey try-out, personally talked to the head coach and met a possible teammate of mine. I pretty much had a permanent smile on my face, sitting in the locker room, which is actually dangerous for a guy to wear. I tried my best to wipe it away so people didn't get the wrong impression.

After removing my skates, I threw them in my duffle bag, put my black sneakers on and started to head towards the exit door. Something didn't feel right; it was as if I was carrying twenty pounds of extra weight on my body. Foolishly, I looked down to see myself still wearing my practice uniform and full padding underneath. I stopped dead in my tracks and just laughed into the air. See what excitement does to me?

2

"Amie, what choo' wanna do? I think I could stay with you, for a while, maybe longer if I do. Ba dum, bum bum ba da bum bum bum bum bummm..."

I knew all the lyrics to the old popular Pure Prairie League song. I mean, come on, I had to. It was, without a doubt, my girlfriend's favorite song and frequently to lighten her spirits, I'd sing the tune to her. I even attempted to learn the chords on an acoustic guitar, but failed miserably. It was the thought that counted, right?

Driving down the highway with my window rolled down, I began to remember the first date Amy and I went on over two years ago. We were merely seventeen-year-old kids, spending the summer between our junior and senior high school years together. We both hung around the same group of friends and began to get close that summer - talking on the telephone late at night and sometimes, sitting next to each other at our group's excursions to the movie theaters. I would always be able to get a good laugh out of Amy, no matter what I said. I could have announced, "Hey! Look—it's a Coke can!" and she'd get a good chuckle. All my friends could tell she had a thing for me (in their words), and I had acquired a slight liking for her. Finally, on the evening of August 6th, 2000, I worked up the courage to ask her out to dinner. I don't remember exactly what was said, but knowing me, it went something like, "Hey, I'm pretty bored. Feel like hanging out?" I quivered the whole time. Right away, she accepted my offer and it turned out to be one of the best nights of my life, capped off by a romantic walk along the Lake St. Clair shore. It had to be around one o'clock in the morning as we lay on the cool sand, looking up at the stars. Amy turned to look at me; I rolled on my side to look at her, and that's where our relationship began. Yes, I know, cue the sappy music now. It was like a scene out of a made-for-TV movie.

Throughout our senior year of high school, everyone called us the perfect couple. I guess we had that look about us. I was the 5 foot 7, wiry strong, athletic person while she was the cute, 5'4", white t-shirt and gym shorts, Volleyball player. Makeup was rarely needed on Amy's face but at formal and semi-formal dances, the lipstick, mascara, blush (and all those other crazy cosmetics girls waste money on) would only enhance her already striking image. During an ordinary day, she normally wore her brown hair back in a ponytail to give her the true high school look. Those were great times.

I guess I can't say our relationship has been perfect, but damn close to it. Every day we were together, it still felt like that first date, like new love. It had been 25 months and amazingly, we were happier now then we had ever been—even with college holding us apart.

It was a short forty-minute drive up route 23 from Ann Arbor, Michigan, to my hometown of Fenton. Even though I'm home basically every weekend, it's always a welcome sight. It's kind of like getting away from it all and going back to the place I know is safe. Plus, I found no reason to stay on campus since I don't consume alcohol (the weekend ritual).

My mother stood on the front porch as I pulled my brown Honda Civic into the narrow driveway. As soon as she spotted the car, she grabbed her pail and pretended to water lilacs on our front porch. The front of our house always looked nice with two hanging plants at the entrance and assorted flowers all around the yard. My mom always seemed to have plenty of time to keep it looking great.

The house itself was in fair condition. It was an elegant sky blue color with gray shutters that badly needed replacing. There were three floors, including the basement, and three bedrooms; perfect for our family. Unlike some families, my brother and I never had to share a bedroom. However, despite this, he'd frequently come barging into my room, especially when Amy and I were in it. Brat.

My mother had opened the driver's side car door before I even shut it off. She was waiting for a hug, which, after I got out, gladly accepted.

"Hey David! Nice to see you!"

"Hi Mom! Is Dad around?"

"Yeah, he's upstairs watching the game with Mikey. How'd the tryout go?"

"I made the cut! But I'll tell you the rest later, maybe at dinner." I hated to cut off my mom, but sometimes it was just necessary—and when the Detroit Tigers are playing baseball, it's necessary.

"Okay honey, do you need some help unloading your car?"

"In a couple of minutes, I'm going to go check on the game." I was halfway inside the house when I finished this sentence. Yes, I confess, I'm a big sports buff. It doesn't just cease at hockey either as I'm a major Detroit Tigers baseball fan. Basically, whatever season it is, I follow the local team in session.

On the present day of the 14th, the Lions were 0-1, receiving a 38-7 thrashing at the hands of the Green Bay Packers, the Red Wings and Pistons didn't start up for another month and surprisingly, baseball's Tigers were stirring excitement in the Motor City. With fifteen games left to play in their season, the club was only 2 games back of the division-leading Indians. In my lifetime, I could never remember the Tigers making it to the playoffs, so needless to say, there was definitely anticipation swirling in the air.

As I entered the TV room, I saw a very familiar sight. My father, sitting on the La-Z-Boy, with a bowl of popcorn in his lap and my seventeen-year-old brother, sprawled out on the couch, wearing gray sweatpants and a dirty white t-shirt. It was an old fashioned lazy Saturday at the Calvetto residence.

"Hey guys!" I said to the two, who were distracted by the television.

"Hey buddy!" replied my dad.

"Yo!" exclaimed my brother, Mikey, never removing his eyes from the set.

"Who's winning?"

"Tigers are up, six to four in the eighth. Looking pretty good," my dad explained, with a Coors Light in his hand. "How'd the tryout go? Did you make it to the next round?"

"You betcha."

"All right!" shouted my father in excitement. "Take it one step at a time, don't burn yourself out in one day. I'm sure they'll see the talent in you, much more so this year than last. You can do it."

The remark took me by surprise. I don't exactly know why but it was just... well, weird.

"Thanks dad."

"Oh hey, Amy called about half an hour ago, she wants you to call her back when you get a chance."

"Is she home?"

"Yeah, I believe so," said my dad, eyes now also glued to the TV.

"Okay, I'll go give her a ring."

I passed through the TV room, towards the long hallway upstairs.

"Aren't you going to watch this? We have the bases juiced here!"

"Uhh, yeah—I'll catch the last inning," I said as I was in such a hurry to hear my girlfriend's voice.

*****

It didn't take long for me to realize the true reason of why I come home on weekends. I stood at Amy's front door, tucking my blonde hair underneath my ball cap, in an attempt to look perfect for her. However, when the door swung open and she stood there, looking beautiful as always, I forgot about my appearance completely. Amy always had that effect on me.

Without a word spoken, we threw our arms around each other and squeezed as hard as we could. Hey, it has only been a week since we last saw each other, but in college years, that has equated to a month. What else is there to do in school, other than daydream? Study? Nah. Hockey was my only remedy.

"Hi!" my girlfriend finally said to me with a big smile on her face.

Today, she wore her straight, brown hair down past her shoulders, just the way I liked it.

"Hey cutie."

We spent some time catching up on things and I got a chance to shmooze with Mr. Lewis (I always enjoyed chatting with him from time to time). I mentioned the hockey tryout to Amy, along with my second week of classes and the new roommate they stuck me with in Ann Arbor. All she discussed was the party she attended the previous night and all the crazy people she met. I just repeated oh cool over and over, feeling pretty damn uncomfortable. It wasn't the fact that she drank occasionally, but maybe that she seemed to get so much excitement out of it. Think of it all—college guys at a party with drunken college girls? The imagination runs wild.

"I wasn't drunk, Dave." Jeez, was she reading my mind?

"What? Oh, well that's good. I mean, as long as you had fun." I breathed a sigh of relief.

"I just like to relax sometimes. I hardly EVER get drunk. And you know I'd never kiss another guy," Amy said with a smirk. Again, relief. I already knew this as she has told me before, but it was great to be reminded.

"I'm not worried about that, you can do whatever you want. I just don't see the enjoyment in it all." I really didn't.

"You're too funny," replied Amy, sarcastically.

She kissed me on the lips and went upstairs to change.

*****

Most people think that I'm the generic jock type. Always clean-shaved, wearing my varsity jacket and baseball cap, with the perfect bend on the brim. I wasn't incredibly muscular but I was strong enough to intimidate the average person (I worked out at the gym between three and five days a week to stay in shape and keep my strength up for hockey season). One wouldn't really notice any serious rips in my body but I knew I was sturdy enough, and that's all that mattered.

People said I had that jock walk going on too. You know, THAT walk. The one where you hold out your chest, tuck your notebooks (or whatever you're carrying) into your side, stick a pencil or pen behind the ear and walk at an off-balanced pace. I guess that described me well, just without the pencil—I never saw the need for that. The funny part is, I'd laugh at other people strutting this way, thinking to myself, *Who's this idiot trying to impress?* I never did it to look good; it just came naturally.

With the jock-type, normally came the jock personality. This was the most stereotypical part of the whole ordeal. Everyone just assumed we traded girlfriends after a few months, cheated our way through school, liked action (on screen or in the bedroom), drank alcohol while underage and many other things. For these reasons alone, classmates would sneer at them, presuming it was all true.

Well, I definitely have a sore spot. Amy and I spent Saturday night at Durgin Park, just north of Detroit on the waterfront. We brought a blanket and lounged on the grass, watching the Summer Theater's production of *Guys & Dolls*. It was a nice, relaxing night out as we strolled along the pier, tossed the Frisbee and grabbed something to eat before the show began. I had a great time and so did my girlfriend. Unquestionably, one of those evenings we'll remember forever.

To my amusement, I saw one of my old high school buddies there, who also used to be considered a jock. Adam Andrews was his name. He skated on the 3rd line of the Fenton High hockey team and played the point on the power play with me. Not to brag, but I was the team's right-winger on the front line and the leading scorer two years in a row. Anyways, seeing Adam at the park got me thinking; what EXACTLY is a jock? Can jocks have long-term girlfriends, attend plays and not feel the need to drink alcohol? And, if so, is he still considered a jock? Do other jocks do the same things as me? Finally, after consideration from the previous statements, is there such thing as a jock? This is what happens when people make silly assumptions.

3

The sun sat high in the bright, blue sky, towering above the massive University of Michigan campus. It seeped into the classroom windows and distracted those wishing to learn. It bombarded into the tallest trees, forming a shadow that stretched forever. It hit the water surface and exploded in all directions in the brightest, white tint you've ever seen. It was a symbol of good spirits all around. It was a famous painting waiting to be drawn and I was doing exactly that. Granted, I'm no artist but sketching was a hobby of mine whenever inspiration struck. And believe me, if this afternoon didn't lift your spirits, than I guarantee nothing ever will.

I sat on a wooden park bench in the heat of midday, my backpack at my feet and schoolbooks by my side. The thick Calculus book sat open with a notebook on my lap, while I pretended to complete a homework assignment. However, I used my mechanical pencil to sketch the scenery of the campus pond and the high-rise buildings that lie before me. From time to time, I would flip back to my "homework" but mostly only when people were strolling by.

Drawing was very soothing for me. I had stacks of paper and even full-length notebooks at home full of doodles of everything imaginable. Unfortunately, I could never sketch something from my mind, which most professional artists could, with ease. But I have to say, while staring at a scene, I could supplicate it quite nicely.

I checked the time on my watch - 1:25. My next class didn't begin for fifteen minutes. Killing time, I leaned back and observed the large grassy area around me where kids were playing a game of Frisbee in the hole, a game I've participated in a few times. I didn't recognize anyone in the shirts versus skins game, as I assumed they were mostly freshman. Along the pond were scattered students (some sitting, some laying on their stomachs) with books open, studying like good college kids do. On two benches, couples sat hand in hand, kissing and cuddling under the warm September sun. It reminded me of Amy and made me miss her even more. There was a time during my freshman year when she came to visit for an extended weekend. Like the couples sitting before me, we too hugged each other tightly on the bench one chilly evening. I had only attended Michigan for over one year but already it had some history for me.

September 27th served as another warm late-summer day in the Southern part of the state. The cold would be arriving soon enough and the students made it a point to enjoy the heat wave while they could. Ann Arbor really *was* a beautiful place to be on days like these.

1:38. I had to go or I would be tardy to class.

*****

Monday's tryout was more intense than that of two days prior. I skipped my 2:45 Calculus class just to stretch long and hard before the 4 o'clock meeting time at the Yost Arena. In addition, I was too excited and had myself quite worked up. Surprisingly, I wasn't as nervous, even though I had never made it this far but went in with more confidence, feeding off of Saturday's experience.

For the full two hours, I worked my ass off, never playing harder in my life. The scrimmage game was about fifteen minutes longer as Coach Trodeau was looking for endurance out of the remaining 36 of us. I skated strong to the finish, netting a pretty goal to put my split-squad up five to four. Unfortunately, when I glanced in the Coach's direction, he was busy chatting with a colleague. Figures.

I came away with only a slight bruise to my left shoulder on a shot to the unforgiving boards. Not bad for the intense level of play. Mentally, I felt good and ended up making the cut. My chances were beginning to look better and better as 24 kids remained and nearly 30 percent of us would make the team. Of course, seventy percent would not.

Tuesday afternoon would be a completely different story. Picture the exact opposite of a perfect performance and that described the 2 hours that late afternoon. It was as if I fell asleep, woke up, and absolutely forgot how to play the game of hockey. I was a lost little child among a sea of giants.

I guess it all started in the first scrimmage game when I got laid out across the ice by an opponent. It wasn't a bone crushing hit or anything as he merely ran into me from behind, but I went crashing down to the frozen surface, sliding violently into the boards. I sat on the ice, stunned at what had occurred and from that point on things would continuously get worse. A pass to me on a breakaway that skipped over my stick and glided to the corner - a three on one break as I stick handled poorly and turned it over to the opposing team - numerous face-offs lost, many offside calls, and even a bit of trash talking, which I didn't expect. It seemed as if I did everything I possibly could, wrong.

Six o'clock couldn't come soon enough in the dreaded Yost. We received the post-tryout briefing by the coach and I was off like a flash into the steamy locker room. I fiercely unsnapped the strap to my helmet, grabbed it by one hand, lifted it off my head and flung it into the front of my locker, causing no damage. I wasn't sure if anyone from behind saw the stunt, but it DID seem to quiet down as if they were observing.

Before working myself in to a frenzy, I decided to sit on the wooden bench and try to calm down. With fists clenched tightly, my eyes were closed and reflecting on my horrific performance. All that I had worked for since I was a little tyke got thrown out the window for another year. There was no way the coach would keep me around, especially for a Big Ten hockey club.

I changed out of my ratty practice uniform and waited. Waited for what seemed like a year, or longer. Waited while others laughed and high-five'd around me. I hoped they would get cut, just so I could do the laughing.

The list didn't have the names of those cut, but rather consisted of the ones still alive (I guess the coach didn't want to single out the losers). When I made my way to the front of the crowd, for some strange reason, I scrolled the names from the bottom up, prolonging the letdown.

Vitek, Strickland, Samuelsson…

The list seemed very short but then again, this WAS the third try-out. It should be down to about fourteen or fifteen.

Norton, Middleton…

DJ Norton was the son of a famous hockey great who skated with the Maple Leafs for fourteen years. I'm a damn walking encyclopedia of sports facts.

Little, Johnson, DeSchriver…

Getting close. It appeared as if only a few names were left.

Collins, Cerulo…Calvetto.

No way. No freaking way. I didn't think about it. I COULDN'T think about it. I silently walked away from the crowd with a stunned look on my face, attempting not to show any joyful signs. I tanked out there on the ice, but the fact of the matter was, I lived to survive another day, in hockey terms of course. Not just another day, but the FINAL day! I waited until I was outside and out of sight to begin my celebration.

*****

"He's just testing me, Mom. He knows I played like crap and wants to see if I can rebound from it and get my game back on Thursday. If I don't play one hundred percent then forget about it."

I spoke into the cordless telephone while lying down on my narrow dormitory bed. It was nearly eight o'clock and the afternoon excitement had worn off. A warm shower did me in as I was already growing a bit tired.

"I'm sorry to hear your practice was lousy. Coach Trodeau must think highly of you if he kept you for the final day." Ah, my mom. Always thinking of the best, trying to keep me in high spirits. I have to say, she was good at it, mainly because I believed her most of the time. "Just erase today out of your mind. The fact of the matter is, you made it to the final tryout and I think you have a good shot of making the team. How many kids are left?"

"Fifteen. Seven make it."

"Well, that's not bad. A little under fifty percent."

"Yeah," I replied, still feeling slightly down.

"Hey, Dave, whether you make it or not, you've done a great job. People won't start thinking less of you if you get cut. You're better than most of the kids out there and you just have to realize that."

"Just 'most'?"

She chuckled. "You know what I mean. There's a famous quote that says, 'If you put your mind to it, you can accomplish anything'. You have to convince yourself that you're the best player on the ice. That way, nothing will stop you."

"Thanks Mom."

"Hey, no charge. I'll be around if you need anything."

Overall, I felt better after the telephone conversation. She always had me believing in myself and I figured she would call me again before Thursday to repeat her encouraging statements.

I had absolutely no homework to finish that night and despite my tiredness, I decided to stop by a friend's room. At the University Of Michigan, no matter what day of the week it was, there was always a party. With an enrollment of over 40,000, it was nearly impossible to discipline the entire campus. This Tuesday evening was no exception.

It was amazing how sixteen people could fit into a dorm room—the size of an average hole in the wall. I counted four on one bed, two on the other and a number of people standing and dancing in the hole's center. As soon as I walked through the door, the room went silent as everyone expected to get busted for underage possession of alcohol. Relieved, a few yelled, "Dave!" as I gave a goofy wave. My friend Elizabeth (Liz) made her way through the crowd and gave me a giant drunk hug. She never hugged me while sober.

"I'm so glad you came! You want a beer?"

"No thanks," I replied with a smirk. I was basically holding my friend up to prevent her from falling.

The dorm room belonged to my friend Justin and some kid I didn't know too much about. Justin attended high school with me and was absolutely living it up in college. Every night a party. However, somehow he managed to pull off the grades, which amazed me.

I knew maybe three or four other people in the room that night, all intoxicated by the twelve o'clock mark. I had a fun time watching and goofing around with everyone, however the real excitement wouldn't begin until the wee hours of the morning.

It had to be 1:30 in the a.m. when Justin and I decided to walk Elizabeth, and her roommate Jen, back to their dormitory. It was a fifteen-minute hike from one residential area to the other, and on top of that, there was a slight drizzle falling. Liz didn't feel safe walking back and hey, I didn't blame her. The long road was very dimly lit and the streetlights were few and far between. One was even flickering on and off. It probably would have frightened *me* if I were alone.

The rain blew directly in my face and stuck to my red, hooded sweatshirt. This forced me to dig my hands deep into my pockets, as chills ran up and down my spine. Despite the atmosphere, my friends continued to enjoy themselves until an unpleasant surprise would soon occur.

There was a sound approaching, similar to the ones we were making. Two, maybe three kids, yelling to each other as if each one was 100 feet away from the other. Drunken conversations. I thought it was humorous myself, but as they sauntered by us, one of the kids bumped shoulders, harshly, with Justin, knocking him off balance. I figured it to be unintentional, however, as I stopped short, Justin strongly believed otherwise.

"Hey asshole!" he yelled, turning around to face the three jokesters. I immediately jumped in front of my friend and held him back with my arms.

"Let them go man, they're just drunk idiots."

"Hey, you wanna fight tough guy?" replied one of the kids through the blinding darkness. I could hear them walking back towards us, which was all I needed, being the only sober guy.

"Justin, let's just walk away."

"What's your problem!?" asked my friend with a violent tone of voice. Before I could turn around, one of the kids had shoved me straight into Justin's chest. I collapsed to one knee and as I got up, saw him chest to chest with my friend, yelling pointless things. They stood about the same height and I knew Justin could kill this kid if he wanted—it was his two friends that I worried about. Hopefully, they would have grabbed the violent one and taken him back to his dorm, however, we weren't so lucky.

"Yo tough guy," said one in a deep voice coming up to me. "You wanna fight?" Rhetorical question of course.

"No, I don't want to *fight*. We're just walking our friends back to their dorm, what's the matter with that?" As I spoke, I spotted an empty bottle of Jack Daniels from his back pocket.

"You guys are lookin' for a fight, come on, let's go!" My enemy whipped off his baseball cap and threw it into my face. "What's the big deal pushin' around my friend, huh? You think it's funny, huh?"

"What!? What's your name?" Instead of answering, I got shoved backwards a step or two.

"Leave him alone!" screamed one of the terrified girls. "Get the hell out of here!"

"Bitch," mumbled the guy in front of me as he extended his arm and half slapped Elizabeth on the shoulder. This scared Jen more than her and made me extremely mad. Drunk or not, this idiot had just laid his hands on a female.

"Jen, Liz, get out of here," I said to them. "Go back to your dorm, we'll take care of this. Go!" Without a word, the girls ran away down the sidewalk. I surprised myself with the sudden burst of authority.

My anger had now peaked and I was ready to hit this kid. The only thing holding me back was the fear that the other two would gang up. Justin had seen this guy push Elizabeth and was now in front of him, yelling heavy, cuss words. Finally, a punch was thrown and the scene got ugly as the third one in the trio came into the mess, violently shoving us around. Justin punched the shortest of the three, square between the eyes, knocking him down to the ground. Being intoxicated, he just laid on the cold, wet sidewalk, as water spurted up from the impact, not knowing what hit him.

The jostling stopped for a second as the two bigger kids tried to help their friend off the pavement. It was like the blind leading the blind, only in this case, the drunk leading the drunk and wounded.

"What's the matter with you!?" yelled the tallest of the three. "Gotta come askin' for a fight, roughin' up my friend. Come on, I'll kick your ass!"

He took two drunken steps towards me and delivered a punch that missed my face. I merely put my hands on his chest and shoved him backward.

"Justin, let's get out of here," I said. "Fighting these idiots isn't going to get us anywhere." Apparently, our enemy had heard the comment.

"What are you, a bunch of faggots? Come on!"

This time, the kid's punch connected right on the left side of my jaw, stinging instantly. I grabbed the collar of his shirt with my left hand and clenched my fist, ready to knock him in the head. My teeth grinded together as I looked into his drunken face, his eyes rolling every which way. I wanted to hit him. I wanted to kill him. He picked a fight with us, he pushed my female friend and he punched me. I was really going to whack him good, maybe draw a little blood and laugh at the stupid fucker while he rolled around in pain. I braced myself for the hit, however, as I started to swing, something inside of me couldn't do it. My fist was frozen in mid air.

With my free hand, I pushed the drunk and grabbed Justin by the arm.

"Let's go."

"Come on, I can kick this guy's—"

"Let's go!" I repeated as we ran away down the sidewalk. I could tell my friend was disgusted, but fighting would have done us no good. Especially, fighting three drunken guys.

"You pieces of crap!" yelled one of the guys from behind us. "Can't even fight...because they're too…much…"

The voices trailed off as we went further down the street. My whole body was shaking, as I now had time to reflect on what had just occurred. I hated myself for being so nervous. But at the same time, I was proud of myself for pulling out of the situation.

We now slowed to a walk down the road as we were far enough away from the drunks to be seen. Justin had sobered up and put his arm around my neck.

"I could've killed 'em, ya know?" he said with a smile.

"I know man. I know."

4

My jaw was swollen for a few days following the early morning scuffle. When sitting around in my dorm room, wasting time, the pain bothered me quite a bit. I'd open and close my jaw, move it in a circular motion and massage it with my thumb, thinking this routine helped. Either way, the pain subsided until around quarter to five, Thursday evening. It took a hard elbow to the jaw for the pain to reappear, only much stronger this time. As far as I knew, the blow came by accident as I was pinned up against the boards with my head down, searching for the puck (always a bad move). After the play, I hunched over and grabbed my jaw with both hands while the culprit said his apologies. After all, it wasn't like he was an opponent.

"Number eight!" came the booming voice from the bench area. "Are we all right?"

"Yes sir! Just aggravated a past injury," I responded. Hey, it was true. Besides, I didn't want to sound like a wuss and get cut for it.

"Do I need to take you out of the game?"

"No, I'm fine Coach!" I would be, later. Much later.

This was two hours of the most intense hockey I've ever played. It was almost as if you forgot about the *friends* you were playing against, and only thought of yourself, doing what it takes to beat them. Luckily, Sean Collins was on my team, as he could surely flatten me.

At 5:30, the whistle blew and I figured the tryout was over.

"Drills! Set 'em up!" yelled Coach Trodeau, as he apparently wanted to see more out of his young players. While others looked winded, I still had plenty of energy bottled up, surprising me a bit.

Jeff Ridley and Richard Hunt set up the orange cones across the ice. Looking like a fashion show, they both wore black wind pants along with matching blue, long-sleeve University of Michigan hockey t-shirts. It looked like the true hockey coach getup with the top-of-the-line, black skates strapped on. I just figured they must shop at the same store.

Two goalies had remained on the final day and I guess the pressure sat heavier on them, especially in the three-on-one and two-on-one drills (the club already had two goaltenders with the option of a third being selected if they excelled in try-outs). After every shift, the two would rotate in and out, trying to better their competitor. This took the heat off of me, at least until I was the defender in the three-on-one attack. I don't recall stopping the offense once in three or four tries—that's why I've always played the wing. Through the years, I was forever the speedy, goal scoring type rather than a big, stand 'em up defenseman. Fittingly, in my eight offensive shifts, I scored twice, got denied once by the goalie and delivered crisp passes the five other tries, setting up nice goal-scoring opportunities.

We moved on to skating drills, which was my forte. I had good speed but could dart around the cones very well. I had been practicing this since the tender age of eight and was more than happy to show off the skills.

Six o'clock came and passed. We were running penalty-killing drills, something I had never seen practiced before. It was basically five men against four for two minutes, like a basic team power play in a regulation game. Being on offense took a lot of hard work, setting up the formation and knowing where to be at all times and the defense simply had to get the puck and throw it out of the zone. I made one heroic move by sprawling out on the ice to block a slap shot from just inside the blue line. I paid the price, though, by getting a puck to the chest.

At ten minutes to seven, Coach Trodeau had seen enough of us and it was a good thing; I began to tire. It felt like the final bell in a boxing match as a pool of sweat occupied my head and bangs and bruises covered my body. I never got that kind of workout in the intramural league—a distinguishing trait between *tough* and *competitive* hockey.

"Hang tight boys, we'll be with you in a minute." I could tell that the coach had his seven players picked. Being one of the tops in the nation, he could instantly notice the strengths and weaknesses of his boys.

The coach and his crew conversed, clipboard in hand, and appeared to finalize some matters before the important announcement.

Surprisingly, I wasn't nervous or jittery. A slight moment of epiphany hit me as I realized, win or lose, I had given my absolute best. And my best was damn good. I could always skate another year with the intramurals, as long as I was playing the game I loved.

Leaning against my upright stick, I heard the 'huddle around' call and glided towards the home team's bench, joining the semicircle of exhausted players. Sean stood next to me, looking winded as sweat glistened from the top of his buzzed hair. I gave him a pat on the back to which he merely responded with a head nod. I returned the gesture.

"All right boys, after careful—What?"

The assistant to his right interrupted the forty seven-year-old coach.

"Yeah…yeah, I got it. No, I got it."

Apparently, Jeff Ridley got humor out of this comment as he flashed his pearly whites. What a funny man. Quit stalling you hilarious comedian.

"Okay, sorry about that. As you all know, my job is especially tough while picking players for my team. Before I read the list of names, I want to say that all of you guys should be proud of yourselves. You played your hearts out for four tough days and that means more to us than just scoring goals. So, a big cheer goes out to you all.

"Those of you who don't make the team let me tell you first off, not to get discouraged. We know who you are and trying out again next year will already give you an advantage above the rest. I highly suggest coming back and giving it another shot. With that being said, I guess it's time to announce the year two thousand-two newcomers to the squad. If your name is called, just skate inside the circle, towards me, and we'll have a quick meeting afterwards." The coach thumbed down his page. "All right…Michael Stutzel…Alex Hutchinson…Derek Strickland…" The names didn't appear to be in any kind of order. "Marc DeSchriver…David Calvetto…Joseph Vitek and Sean Collins. Congratulations guys and we'll see the rest of you next season."

As Sean skated over, we butted fists and smiled at each other. In fact, I ended up butting fists and receiving pats on the back from my other five new teammates, most of whom I hadn't spoken a word to yet. Just a smile dominated my face, as the fact hadn't suck in yet. My mind drew a complete blank.

The little 'meeting' consisted of more congratulatory remarks and the announcement of our first full team practice the following Monday, just a few weeks prior to the October 6th season opener. Amazing to think, I would be in a sparkling yellow uniform with the Michigan logo, skating between thousands of spectators in just under a month.

I began to celebrate at exactly 7:22 p.m.

*****

On Friday evening, a banana yellow University of Michigan flag hung from the front of my parent's porch along with a banner reading, *Congratulations David* with a hockey player's logo on each side. Also, a set of blue balloons flapped around in the wind, tied down to the door handle. The whole array shocked me as it was yet another example of my folks going out of their way. I was always aware that they did a lot for me through the years but probably didn't even recognize half of it.

The front door swung open before I could lay a finger on the bell. The welcoming committee stood there, chatting on the telephone and laughing wildly in a girlish tone.

"Carol, I'm going to have to let you go, Dave just walked through the door. Okay. Yep, you too, take it easy." My mom pulled the phone down from her ear. "Hey!" she exclaimed, excited as she could be with her arms extended in anticipation of the weekly hug. "See that, I knew you could do it!"

"Why thank you," I replied, my head hanging over her shoulder. My body was crushed by her hugging power pressing against my various bruises. "You really didn't have to go through all the trouble."

She simply waved her hand and headed towards the kitchen, looking like a very busy lady. She always attempted to accomplish at least three things at the same time.

"Hi David!" came a voice from my left near the closet, startling me as my body jolted. To my surprise, it was none other than the girl I had fallen in love with.

"Hey! My god, what are you doing here?" I threw my arms around her and delivered a kiss on her cold cheek. To see Amy in my house while I was away definitely *was* a shock. I don't know about her, but I'd certainly feel a bit uncomfortable alone with her father and older brother. *Especially* with her older brother.

"Your mom invited me over for dinner. I just got here about five minutes ago because the traffic was a joke coming up the highway. I left school like three hours ago."

"I thought you had a three o'clock class."

"Yeah, but it got cancelled so I started for home about two thirty." It was normally a two-hour drive from Bowling Green, Ohio to Fenton, give or take ten minutes. I enjoy making the scenic drive down route 41 to see my girlfriend at school.

"Wow! I didn't expect to see you here."

"I can leave if you want," joked Amy.

"No no, I didn't say that was a bad thing." Completely off the subject I remarked, "You look nice tonight." She really did too, wearing a blue, V-neck shirt with a tight pair of jeans. She wore little makeup (as usual) and had her brown hair tied back in a ponytail (again as usual), giving her that high school girl look that I was first attracted to. After two years, my heart still skipped a beat with her by my side.

A large, booming voice came from the living room. "Seventeen innings and they still couldn't pull out a damn win!" Out from the hallway emerged my dad, still dressed in a collared blue shirt and suit pants from the office. His hair jutted out on the right hand side, probably from the stress and him running his hand through it on numerous occasions. Every Friday afternoon, my father looked beat from the week but on this day, he looked more worn out than ever.

"Seventeen innings," I repeated. "What a joke. And to top it off, we lost on a controversial play at the plate! A real bullshit call if you ask me, we had the runner pegged! So now we're four games back of first and Anderson basically tore his leg off. We're so screwed." This severely pained me.

"Oh no!" exclaimed Amy sarcastically. "You mean, you won't have to park yourself in front of the TV to watch the playoffs?"

"Hey come on, we haven't made the playoffs in nine years," I said, defending my team. Girls just didn't understand the whole ordeal. "Hey Dad, thanks for the banner."

"The what?" he asked, looking confused. Not surprising.

"Ah, nothing."

"Congrats on making the hockey team, I had a good feeling you'd be picked.

"Yeah?"

"Yeah. I guarantee, you worked as hard, if not harder than most and you deserved it. I'm sure coming back to try out as a sophomore didn't hurt you either. The Coach looks at that stuff. I'm proud of ya boy."

I smiled. "Thanks."

As we sat around the dinner table that night, the conversation centered on me, something I wasn't accustomed to. Amy felt right at home, joining in on the discussion topic, making jokes and even brought up some news. I could remember the day when she quietly sat at the table, carefully eating her food. It was as if she burst out of her protective shell and became comfortable with my family; not an easy task. Granted, they're both very friendly people but it takes a while to get to know them well.

As my mother rambled on about the hockey team throughout dinner, she began to name the dates of our first few games. Amazingly enough, she knew the schedule up until the beginning of December; while I wasn't even aware of anything past the opening game. Did she really have this much time on her hands?

"We play Colorado College?" I remember asking. "Wow, they're good!"

My parents and Mikey had three weekend home games already penciled in on they're schedules. Something told me, they would soon transform into Wolverine hockey super fans, knowing more statistics than I would. I was thrilled to see my parents so excited and just hoped my playing ability would make it worth the trip. I mean, come on, why drive out to Ann Arbor and buy a ticket to the game just to see your kid warm up the bench?

"We definitely have to come to the season opener," replied my mom somewhere through dinner.

"It's October 6th against Minnesota-Duluth. Their team is pretty weak but the game might sellout. Yost Ice Arena only seats about 6 and a half thousand so you might want to get your tickets in advance."

"Already planned on it." Of course you did.

After enjoying the delightful home cooked meal, Amy and I sat on the living room couch, watching a movie I hadn't seen before. I wanted to change the channel badly but she appeared strangely interested in the mystery flick. I stared at the tube but didn't pay attention to the majority of the movie, making me confused when a climactic scene occurred.

During one of the many commercial breaks, Amy inched up next to me and massaged my swollen jaw with her left hand. It felt so much better than when I attempted to do it.

"Hey Dave," she said, sounding like she was ready to tell me something that was bothering her. "You aren't going to become some cocky jock, are you?"

This comment threw my mind off balance. "What? No, why would you think that?"

"I don't know. I guess I just don't want you to change. You're going to be on a big hockey team now and there's going to be thousands of fans cheering for you every game. I just don't want it to go to your head, you know what I mean?" Her blue eyes looked directly into mine and captured them all too easy.

"Well, there were people cheering for me in high school and I didn't change as a person," I responded, defending my side.

"I know, but this is different. You'll be on TV and everything."

For some reason, this hadn't occurred to me before. "Whoa! Yeah, that's crazy. But I promise I won't change, don't worry."

With her moving left hand, she slightly gripped my jaw, flew in and kissed me on the lips, making my body tingle. We both smiled at each other as I swung my arm around the back of her neck and snuggled up close to her.

The night, as a whole, was rather uneventful but great at the same time. It was near one o'clock in the morning when Amy had to drive home across town. I walked her out onto the front porch, where the wind was whipping around, swaying trees and fiercely flapping the banner in front of me. The rain was pouring down from the sky as we watched the drops smack the driveway and ricochet upwards. Immediately as we were observing, the ropes began to loosen on both sides of the congratulatory sign. It seemed like a slow motion instant replay as the supports wildly unraveled around the beam and the white banner began it's decent towards the soggy grass. We watched it crash in front of us and the wind dragged it further and further away down the drenched front lawn.

"Oh no!"

"It's okay," I replied. "I'll grab it in the morning."

Amy and I said our goodbyes and goodnights, and shared hugs and kisses until she was on her way. I stood at my doorway, watching the headlights of her compact car back out of my driveway. A roar of the engine and she was out of sight, down the main road, a scene I had witnessed many times in the past. No doubt I would see it many times in the future as well.

Thanksgiving Day, 2002

5

"Despite the wind and cold, all these spectators are having a great time here in the Big Apple. Our thermometer has reached thirty degrees with the wind chill factor dropping that number considerably, and forcing the giant balloons to fly lower than normal. Whoa nelly, it takes a lot of strength to be a handler today, but they all look excited to be here.

"Entering Herald Square now is the Sherman Oaks High School Marching Band. The band, consisting of two hundred and seventy kids, has appeared at the Grand National Championships a total of three times and makes their first Macy's Day Parade appearance. Directed by William Tellner, we will hear a Christmas medley comprised of 'Let It Snow,' 'Sleigh Ride,' and 'Rudolf The Red-Nosed Reindeer.' The band sounds great so let's have a listen."

The sounds of the Alabama-based marching ensemble flowed through my living room early in the morning. It was 8:30 central time but it felt much earlier, partly due to the overcast sky keeping the room relatively dark and the fact that I was out late the prior night, cutting into my sleep time. I arrived back home around three o'clock in the AM, exhausted and with a bit of alcohol stored in my stomach. It was quite unlike me but I acquired a taste for sex on the beach just hours ago. They really didn't have too much alcohol in them, mostly fruit juice, but for some reason, it did taste a little funny and had a definite bite to it. Interesting, but tasty nonetheless.

So why was I awake five hours later? Beats me. I jolted upright from a dream that ended about quarter of eight and just couldn't fall back asleep. My father and brother remained in bed with my mom taking her customary thirty-minute shower before preparing desserts for the day, while I lounged on the couch. Feeling no need to be clean, I sat slouched on our sofa, wearing an old T-shirt and sweatpants that were a few sizes too large. My continuously growing hair sat dry and curled up in many spots.

"Wow, they are good, isn't that right Katie?"

"Indeed they are. It's amazing to think that these are all high school kids between the ages of fourteen and eighteen." NBC news anchor, Katie Couric was dressed for a blizzard and wore a big smile on her face. She sat alongside her co-host, Willard Scott, who had been covering the annual Macy's Parade since I was a young kid—and probably before that.

"Well, rolling down the street now comes a fantastic float, titled 'Journey Into Tomorrow.' This futuristic experience features a rocket ship, blasting into new and exciting lands and is the Chairman's trophy winner this year. Riding on the float are children from the local Y.M.C.A and perched up in the large rocket ship stands Grammy-recording artist, Kenny Rogers to spread some holiday cheer."

I started to flip channels when the horrific singing began. If there was one thing I couldn't stand, it was sellout artists, lip-syncing for a televised parade or event. Seriously, it drove me crazy. However, nothing else caught my attention as I found mostly infomercials, news programs and more parade coverage from different spots on the route. "Happy Thanksgiving from all of us here at channel whatever," they all wished.

"What are you doing up?" came my mom's voice, entering the living room in a red bathrobe. Her hair was dripping wet from the shower.

"Morning. I woke up early and couldn't get back to sleep," I told her, not revealing the headache that kept me up. I flipped the channel back to NBC where Mr. Rogers was wrapping up his butchered rendition of 'White Christmas.'

"How's the parade?"

"Same as every year. Although, one of the balloons already had to be deflated. It's so windy that the thing was rolling into the trees."

"Oh no, which one?" My mother appeared ready to laugh.

"I think it was Big Bird." This sent her into hilarity as I started to crack up just listening. She decided to sit down for about ten minutes to keep me company.

"Flying up Broadway, past 38th Street comes the famous smile and colorful clown suit of none other than Ronald McDonald. At forty-four feet high and sixty-three feet long, Ronald returns to the parade for the sixth straight year, although making his debut in 1988. Fifty-five balloon handlers will fly Ronald high above the New York City skyline in an attempt to guide him safely into Herald Square. Katie, I think it's safe to say that these guys aren't clowning around."

For as long as I could remember, Willard Scott was the king of the lame jokes. It brought back memories of past Thanksgiving mornings when I'd be perched on my father's lap, listening to the same fool on TV.

It had been six years since I had a free Thanksgiving morning. All through high school, my friends and I would form a group and go to the classic Fenton High football game. Everyone in town attended the contest as our team always squared off against rival Masterson High for the Pilgrim Bowl trophy. It wasn't the actual game that drove crowds to the stadium but rather to reunite with former classmates and keep a tradition alive. I do, however, recall two years when Lannon Field was packed solid due to the team's stellar record. In both cases, they won the crucial game as the students poured out from the stands and onto the field in celebration. One of the times, I actually got hurt in the stampede but it was all in good fun.

I stayed home that morning for no other reason than I didn't feel up to going. It was colder than most years and I knew from experience that Lannon Field served no protection against the strong wind. Also, by attending school only forty minutes away, I frequently saw my hometown buddies and the game was certainly no reunion.

As the late morning approached, the temperature struggled to pass thirty, forcing me to dig my winter jacket out of the closet. I didn't envy my friends out at the stadium as I sat in a heated car, on the way north for Thanksgiving dinner. My brother and I sat in the backseat of the Ford Taurus, both dressed in polo shirts while our parents were in front, chattering about something they figured to be important. Luckily, my thick headache had subsided thanks to the miracle of ibuprofen. I never thought that just a few drinks could give me that sick feeling but I was wrong. Anyway, it was an hour drive to my grandfather's house up in Palms Point, just long enough to get aggravating every holiday. Mikey always insisted on being a pain in the ass.

Grandpa Calvetto lived alone in a nice, one-story ranch house, only a mile from Lake St. Clair's beach. I imagined it must get lonely, living far away from the family, but he was in good spirits every time we talked. Grandma passed ten years ago when I was a bit too young to understand it all. I just assumed she'd be there the next time we visited but the house was never the same, and neither—I assumed—was her husband.

Joseph Calvetto was now seventy nine years old, had a few gray hairs that still remained above his ears. He was a long-retired accountant but now did volunteer work one day a week at the Palms Point Public Library (quite the tongue twister). Because of this, my grandfather was a familiar face to everyone in town. Mr. Popularity. And boy, did the guy have stories to tell. He'd ramble for hours on end about laboring as a kid, World War II (and basically everything in American History during his lifetime), old Tigers games, antique cars and all else conceivable. Sure, he'd repeat his tales, and change a few things, but it was still great.

Grandpa was the first person to greet our arriving crew through the door.

"Hey hockey star!" he announced with a big smile on his face, ignoring the other three entering.

"Hey Gramp. Happy Thanksgiving."

"Go Michigan! Hey Mr. Hockey! Hey there Hockey Boy," came the voices of the others, apparently delighted to see me. In my nineteen years, I had never received a greeting quite like this. This was shocking as I went to kiss my aunts and shake hands with the uncles around the room. I felt a bit bad for Mikey as only my grandfather immediately welcomed him. Well okay, the feeling passed rather quickly.

My grandfather, Uncle Eddy and Anne had actually attended one of my games during the first half of the season. They were about the biggest fans in the whole arena and since then, have been attached to Michigan hockey.

So I suppose I should briefly describe how the family breakdown goes. We always spent Thanksgiving and Christmas Day with my dad's side of the family up in Palms Point. He was one of three children, two boys and one girl, who are now all married and live scattered around the southern portion of the state. First is my favorite, Uncle Eddy, who is married to Anne, four years younger than him. Ed is the storybook uncle that teaches their nephew how to play golf, takes them skiing and gives them the lowdown on women. He is the baby of the three kids at 39 and was living as a bachelor until three years past.

My Aunt Margaret, 42, was the most conservative. She worked the high-paying yuppie job in downtown Detroit and was married to an accountant, very favorable to Grandpa. Her husband, Uncle Vinny, had a son from his previous marriage and a daughter with Margaret who was nearly nine years old. Mikey and I would always pick on little Christina, basically because we could. Vinny was, at times, very distant from his wife's side of the family. His job ate him up inside making my Uncle appear extremely stressed at every holiday gathering. Vinny often kept to himself and had two sisters, one of which would occasionally join us for Thanksgiving dinner.

Other than the many cousins that my father had, that's the Calvetto family in a nutshell. I hope I didn't leave anyone important out.

Dinner was prepared and set out on the table while the guys watched the Lions play the Chicago Bears on the tube—or should I say losing to the Bears on the tube. We spent the time ridiculing our pathetic football team. I was to the point where I'd pick other teams to cheer on for the remainder of the season.

"Okay guys, dinner is ready. TV off, let's go," came the order from Gramp. The traditional thanksgiving dinner sat on the table: mashed potatoes, yams, stuffing, green beans, corn, squash, gravy and most importantly, a huge cooked turkey in the middle. For ambiance, two large candles were lit at the center of the table and an elegant tablecloth covered the eating area. I sat near the end of the table with Uncle Eddy on one side and Mikey on the other, who would flick food off his spoon at me in years past.

Grace was said and the plates were passed around. I scooped enough food to feed an army, as I was a major fan of the thanksgiving meal. Immediately, the multiple conversations began.

"So did you see that new movie, 'My Wedding Journal'? Everyone was raving about it but I thought it was rather silly."

"How's the job?"

"Wow, Christina is getting so big!"

"Yeah, I saw it. It was decent but not as good as I expected."

"Long hours, not enough pay. You know how it is these days."

"Can you believe she's in the fourth grade now? This kid is shooting up like a weed!" My aunt Margaret turned to her daughter. "Maybe someday you can learn to play hockey like your cousin."

"Mommy, I'm a girl," replied Christina to her mother, making a face (*The Face*, we called it).

"Well, what does that matter?" interrupted my grandfather from the head of the table. "Just because you're a girl doesn't mean you can't achieve what you want to. Your Aunt Mary (Calvetto) says that if you put your mind to it, you can achieve anything. Isn't that right Dave? Tell me, were there any females that tried out for your hockey team?"

"Ah, well no," I said between bites of turkey, killing the motivational conversation. "But the school has one hell of a women's hockey team. They could probably test half the teams in our conference."

"So are you guys in first place?" asked Uncle Vinny.

"We're in second right now. Ohio State is killing everyone so far and we still have to play them three times. I believe they're still undefeated with a tie or two but I know we're four points back of them." (College hockey awards each team two points for a win and one for a tie.)

"That's not bad. How many goals have you scored?" All conversations ceased, as the crowd seemed to be interested in my hockey statistics.

I placed down my spoon filled with mashed potatoes and ran my fingers through my hair, brushing it off of my forehead. "Well, I'm not really sure how many I've actually scored. It's a team effort every game and I just do whatever is possible to help them out. The fans make it so exciting when a goal is scored that it's basically the same feeling whether you're on the ice or warming up the bench." I could tell they didn't buy it.

"How many goals?" asked Eddy from across the table with a smirk.

"Five goals and six assists in fifteen games."

"Wows" were articulated across the dinner table as the relatives believed this to be an astounding feat. Granted, eleven points was pretty damn adequate for a third-line player, especially in his inaugural season, however, I was less than satisfied being a third-line player. My current line mates included two freshmen, one of them a talented center and the other a speedy left-winger. We recorded anywhere from nine to sixteen minutes of ice time a game and lately I had gotten a bit more, being placed on the second power-play unit. Running all this through my mind brought to life the first third of my hockey season. It was nearly surreal as if I was recalling a game I had attended rather than participated in. The intensity of it all never gave me time to sit back and realize exactly what I was a part of. Finally, I did.

*****

"Or the land of the free and the home of the brave."

It was electric. The screaming of nearly seven thousand fans, the blinding lights shining down and reflecting off of the freshly cleaned ice and our opponents, dressed in their brand new brown with maroon jerseys, staring us down, attempting to win the battle of intimidation. The Yost had transformed itself from its original emptiness. Cowbells clang and horns blew. Signs hung across the balcony, encouraging the top players. Vendors yelled "popcorn!" and "get your soda here!" all across the arena. Hats were waved in the air. The band began to blare "Hail To The Victor," a University of Michigan standard, driving the crowd into hysteria as the alums and parents sang along. The student section provided the cheers and the atmosphere; many of their faces painted blue or yellow (or both) and even some wearing clown wigs of the university colors. They occupied four entire sections behind the opposing goal and spilled into the corners. There were absolutely no seats to be had. Mothers and fathers and grandparents and brothers and sisters and students and children and townspeople and alumni and scouts and high schoolers and collegiate coaches and every other possible fan of the program packed the Yost Ice Arena to the ceiling.

And what about me? To put it simply, I was scared shitless. Standing beside our goaltender during the national anthem, I couldn't help but stare all around as I knew the crowd was focused on me. I remembered the days when Dad, Mikey and I would sit in the balcony of Joe Louis and route on our beloved Red Wings, watching every play and critiquing every move. Now I was the one to be judged. Seven thousand Wolverine fans would be staring at ME. And how could I hide it? The name CALVETTO was printed in dark blue with an enormous number fourteen on the back. Not to mention, the genius that designed them made the home jerseys a bright yellow color, sticking out like the proverbial sore thumb. Television cameras were perched atop the first level, pointed at the line of players observing the anthem. I was in the spotlight...and I was terrified.

Looking around the arena, I attempted to spot my folks who informed me they were seated in section 114. All I saw were blue faces, screaming children and a sea of other freaks but no middle-aged couples.

As the horn sounded to start the game and *Guns & Roses* played on the sound system, I took an empty bench spot, next to my buddy Sean. I double checked everything; my skates were tied tight, my pants up to the navel, my jersey was on straight, gloves fastened, the blue helmet on and strapped and my many pads situated in their correct positions. Sean appeared ready to go as if he had been playing collegiate hockey for years. The yellow UM jersey seemed to be made for him.

I leaned over and rapped my stick against the boards to cheer on our boys while the puck dropped. Trodeau started his top line with two seniors, Walsh and Kotti, on defense. Gerry Walsh had won all-American honors the previous year, setting a school record for assists. College Hockey USA predicted him to be a Hobey Baker Finalist this season. Too bad he was an uppity prick off the ice.

The maroon bulldogs from Minnesota-Duluth came out strong and tested goalie, Scott Hooden on a number of shots, but all were swallowed up by the junior. The crowd applauded by yelling "Hooood!!" a name they would frequently call the net minder. Over the first weeks of practice, I had acquired the nickname "Callie," taken from my last name as the coach and crew never felt like yelling the whole thing.

Three minutes gone. The top line received a much-needed rest as I scooted down the bench to make room. Sean Collins was on the ice now along with sophomore defenseman, Marc DeSchriver, who stood 6'1" and was also skating in his first game. They played surprisingly well, stropping the maroon from entering the zone and with 14:21 remaining in the period, dumped the puck down into their end.

"Third line!" yelled Trodeau from behind me. "Third line!" That was I. He called for a line change on the fly and I waited for the right-winger to reach the bench before charging out. Nerves occupied my stomach, but I was focused. Minnesota-Duluth regrouped behind the net and began their strike up the ice as my line entered. Instead of swinging my body around the boards (which I would do every time after this), I flat out leaped onto the ice, losing my footing when my blades smacked the surface. Like a pile of bricks, I tumbled to the wet surface in a most humiliating way.

"Callie! What the hell are you doing!?"

A bit hurt, I leaped to my feet and sprinted down ice, into position. What an embarrassing moment. My teammates would surely poke fun at this one.

Soon after my horrific gymnastics performance, I dug the puck out of a corner and threw it to line mate Alex Hutchinson who shot it over the crossbar and into the crowd, halting play.

Our inexperienced line took the face-off. Alex lost the draw but stole it away from Duluth's center and immediately passed it to my stick. Standing seven feet from the goal, I snapped a wrist shot that sailed wide right.

"Damnit!"

"Chump!" yelled an opponent, trash talking.

From that moment on, the third line continued to dominate in surprising fashion during our first game. The enemy never had the puck in our zone and I felt like a winner when skating off the ice. I had nearly forgotten my crowd-pleasing fall from minutes earlier. That is, until I hit the lockers following our victory.

*****

"So you really fell down when you jumped on the ice?" asked little Christina with eyes wide open.

"Yep, I did. Pretty embarrassing, huh?"

"Hahaha!" Christina, as well as the family, got a good chuckle out of my story. Being two months from the time it happened, my teammates still frequently brought the event to my attention. However, my fall took a backseat to star-player, Gerry Walsh, and his escapade during the first week of November.

Our team was visiting Northern Michigan and we were participating in our routine skate prior to the game. Gerry, who was skating in circles around our goal, was chatting with friend, Eric Lessard, at the same time. Neglecting to glance in front of him, Gerry collided into the net as he fell hard to the ice and dragged the obstacle around with him. The team laughed for hours on end regarding this one but Gerry was a bit more sensitive than I. Luckily, the skilled defenseman didn't suffer any injuries and ultimately threw it back in NMU's face by scoring a goal and recording two assists.

I reached across the table and forked myself three pieces of white turkey meat.

"So Mikey," started up Eddy from the far right side of the table. "How's your senior year treating you?"

"Good." My brother didn't elaborate.

"You playing any sports this year?"

"Just soccer."

"Hmmm," thought our uncle. "You never had the desire to take up ice hockey, like your brother?"

"Nope. Never was much good at it."

"So are you thinking about playing soccer in college, wherever you end up?"

"Maybe." Mikey didn't seem to be in a very chatty mood.

"Mike, you suck at soccer," I added sarcastically.

"Shut up! I'm a starting forward on my... What the hell do you know about soccer anyway!?"

"Hey!" said my father from next to me. "Leave your brother alone."

I leered at him to which he didn't find humorous.

Grandpa Calvetto began to ramble to his children about stocks and I quickly lost interest. Thinking about our upcoming trip to Boston, I began writing down statistics in pencil on my napkin. From December 1st through the 4th, our team would travel to the northeast for three tough, non-conference games. The Wolverines would face-off against Northeastern and then Boston University twice, in that order. Three games in four nights would be tough enough without adding the distance traveled from home. But I felt confident in our squad; currently, as I mentioned, the squat sat in 2nd place with a record of 10 wins, 3 defeats and 2 ties. The standings as of November 24th looked like this:

Ohio State	12-2-3	27 pts
Michigan	10-3-2	23 pts
Michigan St.	9-6-1	19 pts
Alaska-Fairbanks	8-3-3	19 pts
Notre Dame	8-7-2	18 pts
Lake Superior	8-9-0	16 pts
Northern Michigan	6-11-1	13 pts
Bowling Green	6-12-1	13 pts
Western Michigan	6-12-0	12 pts

Nebraska-Omaha	4-11-1	9 pts
Miami (Ohio)	2-9-4	8 pts
Ferris St.	2-14-1	5 pts

"Hey Dave, how's that girlfriend of yours? Amy is her name?"

"She's good, thanks," I replied to my aunt. "She's running track down at Bowling Green, has to go back early this weekend for a meet.

"Oh no kidding. You two have been together quite some time now."

"Two years and a little over three months."

"She's such a nice girl," beamed Aunt Margaret.

"Yeah, too bad she's so unattra…"

"Shut up Mikey!" I retorted. "Nobody cares for your ridiculous opinion!"

"Mike, what is wrong with you today?" whispered my mother, loud enough for the entire table to hear.

"May I be excused?" he asked.

"No."

6

Winter was most undoubtedly upon us. The leaves were shook completely from the trees and the temperature was bone-chilling cold, colder than most years it seemed. I had purchased a new, thick winter jacket the previous month and was forced to make good use of it this evening.

The sun set about five o'clock that Thanksgiving afternoon. When stopping at the house for a brief minute, there was a message on the answering machine, waiting for me:

"Hello, this message is for David. This is Coach Ridley calling to inform you of a practice Saturday at four in the Yost. Remember, we have a home game Sunday night and it's up to Coach Trodeau whether we will skate around that morning. If

you can't make practice on Saturday, please call me in the athletics department at 473-551-2332. Enjoy your holiday break and I'll see you Saturday."

Wonderful! That meant my thanksgiving vacation would be cut down by a day. It was at this point in the season where the team began to despise practices and simply wanted to play competitive games. However, as the old saying goes, practice makes perfect. We would do anything to achieve first place. I would make certain to arrive early to boot as I was still attempting to make a good impression with the coach. Rumors were also looming regarding bumping me up to the second offensive line—the coach needed to know I could handle it, so my work was cut out.

Around 6:30, I made my way to Amy's residence for dessert as promised. Her extended family was just leaving as I arrived and a few of her friends were sitting in the living room along with her father and grandmother.

I let myself in the front door and voiced my greetings to everyone.

"Hey Dave, Happy Thanksgiving!" welcomed Amy's father while getting out of his chair. "Let me take your coat."

"Hi David, good to see you!" exclaimed one of her high school chums.

"Hiii Daaave!" That would be Carla from the end of the sofa. She also went to high school with the both of us and held an extremely heavy crush on me for way too long. She obviously hadn't changed a bit since graduation, wearing a pound of makeup on her face and large hoop earrings. Her hair was long and curly, which she had tied up into a bun and she wore an elegant black top with a dark green skirt that hung to her knees. On her feet sat an unpleasant pair of black high heels that were screaming to be removed. I couldn't help but chuckle to myself. Granted, Carla was a genuinely nice person but I never saw myself suffering through a relationship with her. Not only would I be miserable, my reputation would be tarnished. It made me appreciate Amy that much more.

"Carla, how the hell have you been?" I asked jokingly.

"Oh, I'm gooood. Amy and us girls were just talking about you. We all wanna come to UM and see one of your hockey games. Wouldn't that be cooool?!"

"Superb."

"Amy says you're doing reeeally well. I can't wait to see you in action."

I laughed. "Relax, I'm not that good but our team is."

Amy's father began to speak to his 82-year-old mother. "Mom, you remember David, right? He plays hockey for the University of Michigan now and is doing quite well."

"Of course I remember Davie. It's very nice to see you again." Her voice was very muffled and raspy.

"Good to see you Mrs. Lewis."

"Wow Dave, your hair is getting so long and bushy!" butted in Carla. "It makes you look so much different!"

I ran a hand through my thick hair to brushing it back. "Different as in good or different as in horrible to look at?"

"No, I like it! It gives you that real college guy look." Whatever that meant.

Thankfully, it was then that Amy trotted into the living room, carrying one of her cats in her arms. She wore a casual blue dress and was barefoot walking along her spotless carpet. Her brown hair was surprisingly down, hanging a few inches below her shoulder blades. She looked strikingly beautiful as we kissed each other with the spectators looking on.

"Awwww."

Carla and her gang would only stick around for an hour but she made the most of it. By the time she departed, I couldn't stand to hear the resonance of her voice anymore. She had us knee-deep in a story regarding her latest boyfriend from school who sounded like quite the asshole.

"We met at a party and everything, right, and he was like the sweetest guy in the world. He used to bring me flowers like randomly and all and everything was going fine until he claimed that he was going home for the weekend." Amazingly, she said this in one gigantic breath. "WELL, he comes back Sunday with two huge hickeys on his neck. So I was like, 'What the hell is that?' The idiot tried to tell me he banged his neck twice moving furniture for his mom. So I was like, 'that's the worst lie I've ever heard!' But stupid me, I decide to give him another chance and the next weekend I catch him kissing another girl! How do I meet these people, I mean seriously, is something just wrong with me?" Carla actually got misty-eyed over her rather funny story, slightly smearing makeup below her eyes.

The four girls present that evening were such an odd combination to say the least. First there was Amy, the very outgoing, athletic type who was always busy with something. Justine and Sarah had been two of her best friends since elementary school, both of which were extremely shy and excelled in grammar school, carrying on to college. Neither played sports or participated in any time-consuming activity. And then there was Carla. Well, no words could truly describe this girl. Regardless, the four amigos did everything together and were some of the closest friends I've ever seen.

After the girls left, I ate two pieces of apple pie, which were graciously offered to me at the kitchen table. Mr. Lewis and Amy sat with me as we reminisced over past events and eventually, the present. Her father seemed very interested in attending an upcoming hockey game, as I never realized how much of a fan he was.

"Yeah, the game was broadcasted on SportsStation Eleven last weekend so I had a chance to watch."

"Was that the Northern Michigan game?" I asked, trying to remember our schedule.

"I believe so."

"I played a pretty horrible game that night. I just didn't have it."

"Well, it looked like you were skating pretty well. You had their defense beat on a number of occasions."

"Ha ha, their Swiss cheese D?"

"Well, I'll tell you something, you guys play like one of the best college teams I've ever seen." Amy's father removed his eyeglasses and cleaned them on his shirt. "So tell me, do you guys ever break into fights like the professionals?"

"Not normally, however, it's happened once this year, unfortunately."

Unfortunate in the fact that suspensions were handed out to our star athletes. It all started with one jackass defenseman from our non-conference rival, Wisconsin, who insisted on taunting and shoving around our guys all night, most notably our first-year player, Derek Strickland. He was getting pushed after the whistle on numerous occasions but the worst was yet to come. Late in the final period while skating off the ice prior to a face-off, our Wisconsin friend shot a racist remark towards the African-American, Strickland, and all hell broke loose. From the bench, the scene was an explosion of sticks, gloves and helmets. Everyone in a hockey jersey, whether white or blue, raced to the far corner where the fight was rapidly intensifying. I followed suit with my bench-warming buddies and leaped over the boards to back up our teammate. Sean Collins threw punches left and right to any bruiser unlucky enough to be sporting a white uniform. With my heart pattering, I got to the center of the brawl and bear-hugged a couple of Wiscy players in a restraint attempt. Not the smartest move. I didn't dare take swings at anyone due to the fact I'd be drilled into the ice faster than the referees could save my pathetic self. Actually, I was more afraid of a flying object coming out of the crowd and pelting me square in the head. The fracas drew them into frenzy, throwing cups, bottles, magazines and anything in hand at the visiting team. That happened to be us.

Thankfully, the referee and both linesmen broke up the fight before players were seriously injured. Ed Blackwell, the team trainer, would examine a few of us, just for precaution's sake.

"Number twenty-four and number five, five minutes each for fighting and ten minute game misconducts," voiced the referee with the orange stripe on his arm. "Get them out of here."

In collegiate play, a game misconduct meant an automatic ejection from the game. Strickland was first to go and Walsh followed as Coach Trodeau shot them both a nasty expression, "Learn how to restrain yourself boys!" Assistant Coach Ridley patted his men on the back.

"Number forty-nine, five minutes for fighting," continued the Zebra, indicating Sean's number, "and number fourteen, two minutes for roughing." Well how about that. My first ever penalty. All I tried to do was break up the situation but the biased referee threw me in the box.

After the game, it was nearly impossible for the team to refrain from hysteria when confronted by Trodeau. It was great for the squad to defend our teammate but the contest turned into a circus and the coach couldn't have been pleased with the two, two-game suspensions.

As I recalled the events of that night, my lips curled upward.

"I know what you're thinking about," remarked my girlfriend.

"Hey, it was funny," I answered, turning the discussion to a private one. Her father just smiled.

"It was not funny, you could have gotten seriously hurt. Did that thought ever cross your mind?"

"Nope."

Sarcastically, she rolled her big, blue eyes. "What a surprise."

"Hun, I'm a hockey player. Skirmishes like that are going to happen all the time. Maybe they won't all be to that extent, but it's all part of the game. I won't let our boys be tossed around like that." A true hockey player, I was evolving into.

"He's right, you know," chimed in a wise Mr. Lewis. "How are your parents, Dave?" he asked, changing the subject.

"Oh, they're good, busy as usual. Good pie by the way, did you make it yourself?" I placed my hand on Amy's leg underneath the wooden table.

"Believe it or not, I did."

Gibson Lewis was a good, kind-hearted man. When the divorce with his wife occurred four years previous, Amy stayed at the three-bedroom house in Fenton with her mother. For two long years, my girlfriend suffered through this living situation until she turned 18. Her father, now living in a 2-bedroom townhouse in East Fenton, was more than delighted to take his daughter in. She stayed here now every weekend when home from school.

Since Amy departed the old house, Mrs. Lewis moved south down route 41 to Dundee with her new fiancé. I was still unsure if they were fully married so I would just assume so. In that case, she moved down south with her new husband. It was an awkward situation from my perspective, coming from a happily married family who all resided under the same roof.

Gibson was now pushing fifty years old and nearly all the hair on his head had turned to gray. He normally wore a thin pair of glasses that rested above his bushy moustache, an appearance that had him look younger than actually was.

"Can I get you anything else Dave? We have plenty of leftovers," voiced Mr. Lewis.

"No thanks, I ate enough food for a week today." I really did.

"Well, I'm going to clean up a bit, make yourself at home."

Amy waited until her father had vacated the kitchen before spilling what was on her mind.

"David, I'm worried," she blurted, looking me straight in the eye. I knew she wasn't kidding, using my full name and everything. I couldn't imagine what the problem was.

"What's the matter babe?"

"I was talking to Matt at this morning's football game." Immediately, my heart skipped a beat. "He was telling me about last night. You guys had a good time?"

"Ah, yeah. I guess. It was good to see all the guys again." Matt was one of our joint-friends from high school. He attended the local community college outside our hometown and still lived at home with the folks.

"Matt told me you were drunk!" exclaimed a stern-faced Amy, lips tight and eyes staring. I went pale. Quick, think of a response.

"No! No, no," I started. "No, I just tried a few sips of the mixed drinks they were making. Matt insisted that I at least try the stuff. It was pretty horrid if you ask me."

Oh my god. I was lying directly to my girlfriend's face and was actually starting to believe myself. "I couldn't stomach more than half a cup of any kind." The truth was that I had not totally reached the drunken state (at least I didn't think), but was buzzing pretty heavily and it wasn't the first time. The worst part was, I was unsure why I had to lie about this. It wasn't as if this was some huge deal.

"I like mixed drinks," blurted Amy, taking me completely by surprise. "Especially grape juice with some vodka in there."

"I'll just take the grape juice," I said lightly. Now, I completely forgot the blatant lies escaping from my mouth—I was just rolling with the conversation.

"Well, you know I don't care if you decide to drink alcohol," returned Amy to the subject at hand. "Just don't try and hide it from me."

I knew that she could read straight through me.

"Don't worry honey, I wouldn't do that."

*****

Mikey had gotten sick late that thanksgiving night. The big dinner must have been churning in his stomach, and due to that, I decided to drive home before midnight to help him out. It was quite unlike me to leave the Lewis household before the early morning hours.

As I departed out the side door, Amy escorted me to my little, rundown Honda Civic and hugged me like never before. She grabbed on tight around my waist and lightly kissed me on the neck.

"I'll see you tomorrow before I leave," I whispered to her.

"Okay. I love you."

"Love you too."

Waving goodbye, I backed out of my visitor's parking space and sped down the road, en route to the highway. Fenton was a dark and lonely place during the middle of the night. There was nearly no activity on the streets, people or cars.

I flipped on the radio, cycling through some of the local stations.

"...Forming a low pressure system in the northern portion of the state. Tomorrow's highs will only reach thirty-five in the Detroit metro area and the weekend looks sunny but cold."

I tuned the radio up a few dials.

"...That's why, darling, it's incredible, that someone so unforgettable, thinks that I am...unforgettable, too."

Too old.

"Another forty minutes of soft rock is coming right up on The Stream, 105.5." This would do. I placed my hand back on the steering wheel as the clock struck 12:00.

December 2002

7

It was early on Thursday morning when the team's prevost bus pulled into Boston's Ramada Inn. On this December 1st, the weather couldn't have been much warmer than that of southern Michigan; the wind made it a numbing cold as winter parkas, leather jackets, hats, sweatpants, thermals, and boots covered our freezing bodies. Luckily, we would have a few hours of rest in the Ramada before the bus would take us downtown to Massachusetts Avenue.

Over these four days, our now third place Wolverines would play three games against two tough hockey east opponents. First, the sight would be Matthews Arena for a contest with the Northeastern Huskies. Then Saturday and Sunday nights would feature two marquee match-ups, as our squad would invade Walter Brown Arena to take on the feared Boston University Terriers.

It was a long weekend away from Ann Arbor. Most of us, including myself, had term papers to complete due the beginning of the next week. We would miss class the Thursday and Friday but school athletes were always excused without a quandary—that card would be played more than once.

The weekend trip was, surprisingly, my first visit to Boston, Massachusetts. Actually, I had never been to New England at all. Our bus had arrived in the early morning hours so I couldn't make out the sights through the darkness but I had hoped to take a stroll through town during our free time on Friday.

Thursday was a grueling afternoon, filled with two hours of practice, a lunch break, two more hours of practice and a game that evening. We got a 60-minute rest before the face-off to eat and get changed into game time attire. And while some of us were still a bit tired (like myself), most were filled with energy; fighting for a top spot in the division most definitely aided in that aspect.

Prior to our pre-game skate, I napped on an old, uncomfortable wooden bench in the visitor's locker room. Matthews Arena was an extremely aging facility. It acted as home to the Boston Bruins back in the early 1900's and hasn't exactly been renovated since. The barn made the Yost Ice Arena look like a palace with endless amenities. So when I say that I napped on an old, uncomfortable wooden bench, it's no exaggeration.

The 3,500 seat arena would be uncommonly full that evening. I assumed most people were there to see a rare appearance by the Michigan Wolverine hockey team as the hometown Huskies were sitting dead last in their division. In fact, Northeastern only held two wins thus far in the season against weak opponents, Niagara University and division rival, Merrimack. Our team was already preparing for the weekend series, but like most top squads, couldn't look past the game at hand. As history proves, that's when the biggest upsets tend to occur.

I awoke to the alarm on my wristwatch at 6:12PM and immediately suited up. We wore the blue uniforms with yellow pants tonight, our customary away jerseys. The number 14 with the name 'Calvetto' was printed in a lemon yellow on the back.

To my surprise, Coach Trodeau called for a conference in the locker room before invading the ice. Only once before had he done this and it was months ago on opening night.

"Alright boys, gather 'round." I took my place on one knee with Sean on my left and Alex to the right. "Is anybody tired?" asked the large, authoritative coach. Few raised their hands, as I didn't dare show mine. "It's alright, I'm a bit lethargic myself. All I ask is that you give me three periods of excellent hockey, then we can go back to the hotel and get a good night's sleep."

Boy, how I'd love a good night's sleep. "Now, as for tonight's game, Northeastern has been preparing for us since September. They've had a rough year so far but I'm sure they're stepping up their game tonight. SO, I'd better not see any lackluster performances out there. Got it?" We uniformly nodded our heads. "Alright then. The third line gets the start tonight with Gerry (Walsh) and Tom (Kotti) on defense. Let's have a quick 'Wolverines' on three. One, two, three—."

"WOLVERINES!!"

Alex and I butted fists, as our line would start for the first time all season.

"On the ice boys! Face-off is in thirteen minutes!"

*****

The expected crowd all showed up that frigid night in the center of Boston. The cold weather didn't just cease outside either, for Matthews was one of the coldest college arenas in the states. Being decades old, no heating system was installed as fans braved the temperatures by dressing warmly.

At approximately five minutes prior to the drop of the puck, the public address announcer boomed over the loudspeaker, and the two teams lined up on their appropriate sides.

"Good evening fans and welcome to tonight's match between the Michigan Wolverines, and your—Northeastern Huskies! A reminder to all fans to beware of flying pucks throughout the course of the game and that any spectator interfering with play will be arrested and subject to prosecution.

"And now the starting lineups, first for the visiting Wolverines. Playing left wing, a sophomore from Toledo, Ohio, number twenty-nine, Alex Hutchinson." Alex skated up to the blue line, helmet tucked under his armpit. "At center, a freshman from Battle Creek, Michigan, number forty-one, Michael Stutzel." Stutz followed Alex, amidst the light boos, and halted to his right. "On right wing, a sophomore from Fenton, Michigan, number fourteen, David Calvetto." I skated out to the blue line in undeniably one of the greatest moments of my lifetime. "On defense, a senior from Toronto, Ontario, number thirteen, Tom Kotti and a senior from Peoria, Illinois, number five, Gerry Walsh. And in net for Michigan, a senior from Alberta, Canada, number thirty-five, Scott Hooden." The six of us stood at the blue line, slapping fists (all except for big shot Gerry, of course). "Head Coach for the Wolverines is Jerry Trodeau along with assistants, Jeff Ridley and Red Blemenson."

The lights went out in Matthews Arena as the home team was introduced. I was familiar with the player's names due to the scouting report we participated in the day before. Friday evening would be spent preparing for Boston University.

After we stood motionless while observing our nation's anthem, I strapped my helmet on tight and skated in three donuts before setting up to the right of Stutz at the center-ice red line. I stared down Northeastern's left-winger, positioned before me. Actually, he said to me:

"Hey fourteen, how was the trip over?"

"Not bad," I replied to the more slender opponent wearing the number 12. "Long drive."

"Yeah man, I hear that. Well, good luck to you."

"Likewise."

And from the drop of the puck, we played like mortal enemies, simple as that.

Stutz controlled the opening face-off and threw the puck on my stick as I cleanly handled it. WHAP! Number 12 for the Huskies checked me in the ribs but ended up falling on the ice, rather than me. I regained control on the right side.

"In front!"

I fed the puck to Hutchinson's rapping stick as he danced around a tall defenseman and shot it high, over the net.

"Damn it!"

Merely twenty seconds into the contest, I put the skates in high throttle and raced behind the net to gather possession. I beat my counterpart to it, wristing a shot that skipped off the boards and landed between Gerry's legs at the point. Being an all-American, the buff player instantaneously fired a pass cross-ice to Kotti. Northeastern was already scrambling around in their defensive zone, pointing and yelling at teammates.

"Box Formation! Box! Box!" Trodeau yelled from the bench. We practiced this setup extensively.

"Callie!"

Tom drove a pass straight from the blue line to the end of my outstretched stick. I had my back turned to the net when—

"Ugh!" I was blindsided by the tall defenseman who threw me backward but failed to steal the puck. Using all my strength, I kept my balance, reached out and passed the stone to Michael, who stood five feet from the opposing goalie. "Mike! Coming in!"

The freshman turned perpendicular to the goal and one-timed a wrist shot, flying in mid-air that dinged the right crossbar and sailed into the back of the net. The Husky goaltender threw his stick to the ice as he yelled a few obscenities.

Our five in blue jerseys threw up our arms in celebration and formed a circle around Mike.

"Yeah brother!"

"Hell yeah! Beautiful!"

We all skated back to our bench in a single file, straight line, hitting the extended hands of our delighted teammates.

"Alright, alright. Way to go! Line one!" yelled Trodeau, wasting no time.

As the top line took the face-off, Alex, Stutz and I sat side-by-side on the bench, conversing over the sweet goal. We had already taken the capacity crowd out of the game.

"University of Michigan goal scored by number forty-one, Michael Stutzel, assisted by number fourteen, David Calvetto and by number thirteen, Tom Kotti. Stutzel, number three on the season, by Calvetto and Kotti. Time of the goal, fifty-seven seconds of the first." It was our quickest goal scored all year.

Before Northeastern could regroup and gain momentum, Sean Collins hummed a slap shot from the blue line which slapped off the goalie's pad and got tipped in by a diving Eric Lessard. The crowd booed wildly, as their home team trailed by 2, merely 90 seconds in. The annihilation was on.

Our hard-working 3rd line played more shifts over the three periods that night, maintaining the strong advantage throughout. With a 4-0 lead and two minutes remaining in the first, our line and the 2nd defensive unit (Collins and DeSchriver) were called upon. The puck sat behind our goal as I leaped over the boards (nearly loosing my balance AGAIN) and waited for the defense to gain control. Northeastern countered with their top line, those of which allowed the first goal to sail into the net.

Our five skated the puck up to mid-ice, controlled by Stutz, with Alex and I on either side. He passed the puck to his left where racing in at high speed, I crashed into a Husky player, sending him propelling backward. Forgetting the play in his zone, the opponent appeared ready and willing to retaliate. I positioned myself ten feet from the net and hollered for the puck when—

CRASH! The defender checked me in the ribs with his stick turned sideways. Sweat exploded off my face as I lost my balance and tumbled to the hard, cold surface with a driving force. Luckily, my pads allowed me to hit the ice and bounce a few feet back up. It still wouldn't prevent the pain.

As I struggled to get to my feet, the center, Stutzel, gave the Husky defenseman a hefty shove to his chest.

"Mike! Forget him!" My plea was too late. The head referee, standing right next to the incident, blew his whistle.

"Number forty-one, two minutes for roughing!"

Stutz didn't seem at all pleased regarding the call.

"Bullshit ref! Get the call right! Why don't you open your eyes, huh?!"

"Easy son!" retorted the referee. "Or I'll give you a misconduct. Take your two minutes and get in the box."

Mike mumbled a few more nasties under his breath and accepted defeat.

"Calvetto, Collins and DeSchriver, stay out!" yelled Trodeau with 80 seconds left in the period. "Strickland, your on center. Calvetto! Take the wing!"

Derek and I had never played the penalty kill together and with a

4-0 lead, we'd be able to feel each other out. Northeastern seemed frustrated by looking in their eyes and weren't exactly in a rush to commence the below-average power play. It seemed as if the opposing coach closed his eyes while selecting his five for the power play unit—they used five forwards, three of which were first-year players.

The clock began to tick as Strick lost the face-off to a pesky Husky. We dropped back in the penalty-kill formation; Strick and I up front, Sean and Marc hanging back. Northeastern countered with two at the point and three deep in the zone, guarded heavily by our two defensemen.

Number six of the Huskies controlled the puck on the far side. He handled it until he liked what he saw and passed it horizontally to the forward-turned-defenseman, whom I was covering.

"Back! Back!" He slapped the puck off his stick and sailed it back across the ice. They started this two-man game attempting to lull us into sleep. When another pass glided over in my direction, the converted forward winded up his stick.

SLAP! He took a one-time shot that connected perfectly off the black taping. Without hesitation, I sprawled down sideways on the ice, turning my head away from the flying object. The puck slapped my kneepads at full speed.

"Yes! Nice block Callie!" I felt quite satisfied with myself, considering I've always wanted to block a hard slap shot in a competitive game.

While leaping up, I noticed the puck, which ricocheted off my pad, squirting down the ice at an odd role. Derek Strickland got an early jump on it as no Husky player was within 15 feet of the streaking forward. Strick flew in on the breakaway, untouched. There came the wrist shot. Score! I, again, raised my arms in midair to celebrate our 5th tally of the period.

The boos were really raining down on the lowly home team. At the close of the first, we clambered through the tunnel, trying to wipe the laughter away. We held a five-goal lead, as the spectators were less than thrilled about paying the admission price. The Wolverines stormed into Boston and viciously attacked the Huskies.

"Did you see those two little, skinny forwards crash into each other?" joked the large Ben O'Connor at high volume.

"Ha ha! These guys are horrible!" answered Gerry. "My old pee wee team could beat the shit out of them! I could put my *grandmother* on skates and *she* could beat the shit out of them!"

"They shoot like pee wees too," chimed in Hooden, who stopped all 7 shots he faced; none difficult.

Backup goalie Marcus Pellenisius (nicknamed King Marcus) added, "Coach will put me in before long, yes?"

"Probably. You could use some work."

Sean and I boomed aloud at the humorous conversations. Even *we* didn't realize how truly easy it was to defeat this team.

"Well, at least people in the area know we're a championship caliber team," spoke Sean while clearing the perspiration off his buzzed hair.

"That's for sure. I hope BU (Boston University) is watching this."

Totally off the subject of the game, Sean mentioned, "Man, I can't wait to get back home."

"Why's that?"

Sean, busy re-lacing his skates, didn't appear to hear me. "I'm sorry, what's that?"

"Why can't you wait to get back home?"

"Oh, I have tons of schoolwork to do and all. I haven't seen my girlfriend in, like, a week either."

"Does she go to UM?"

"No man. She's a sophomore at Notre Dame, real smart girl."

"Notre Dame, huh? That's quite the drive."

"Eh, it's not too bad. I'm lucky to have her. Are you seeing anybody?"

"Yeah, she goes down to Bowling Green," I started to say. "Hey, I can't be talking about this! I'll lose my focus!"

Sean laughed. "Sorry dude."

Trodeau had to settle his boys before the start of the middle period. Right about then, we were twenty of the cockiest college kids alive.

At one point during the 2nd period, I overheard seniors, Ben O'Connor and Jeff Thomas, conversing over the stock market. The stock market! Two talented athletes on a championship contending team talking about bears and bulls! The humorous part was, as soon as Jeff Thomas' 2nd line took the ice, he netted the 7th goal of the game, seeming completely alert.

Our team went on to win by a count of 10-1 that evening with Northeastern's lone goal coming on a screen that slid past Marcus in the final period. Line mate Stutzel finished with two goals along with Strick (our epithet for Derek). Walsh, Thomas, O'Connor, Vitek, DeSchriver and Lessard had one apiece as I collected three assists; one each frame. For being exhausted at face-off, I was surprisingly on my game all night. Hopefully, it would carry over to the weekend and ultimately, the rest of the season.

The two opposing teams shook hands following the final buzzer. Mostly all of Northeastern's players were friendly, congratulating us on a game well played. Number 12 was once again my friend. He wished the team and I the best of luck into the New Year and even said, he'd route us on in the playoffs. Maybe it was thinking too far ahead, but he was a nice kid, nonetheless.

Skating off the Matthews Arena ice surface, I noticed a few local cameramen, scrambling around for interviews. I passed through the bench area just at the right second as one of the men dressed in suits stopped me and asked for a quick word. Feeling pumped up after the thumping, I easily agreed.

"Thanks son, we appreciate it."

"Oh, it's no problem." I was still fully dressed in the blue UM jersey with helmet off and bushy hair draped over my damp forehead.

"Alright, this is New England Sports Network out of Boston. As soon as I get the 'OK' upstairs, we'll be ready to roll. Let's just position yourself up against the wall here." I wondered how many professionals could get accustomed to this. By the way, this was my first ever television interview.

The interviewee put his finger to his ear and nodded to the cameraman, signaling to start taping.

"OK John, we're here with Michigan forward, David Calvetto, who recorded three assists in tonight's contest. Thanks for joining us Dave." The reporter threw the microphone in my face.

"My pleasure."

"We here in Boston aren't too familiar with the CCHA. Tell us, if you could, Michigan's key to success so far this year." Quite the heated question to begin.

"Well, it's a number of things," I started to answer. "We have a good core of four or five graduating seniors on this team that are experienced and provide much leadership. Guys like me have learned a lot from them and have molded into the structure of the team. Due to that, our third and fourth lines have been very strong on top of the great goal scorers like Eric and Gerry. Plus, we have the Hoover in net and a wise, veteran coach. All that added together will chalk up a few wins."

"And the Wolverines have gotten more than just a few wins this year as the victory boosted you to second place in your division. Let's talk briefly about tonight's game and the utter destruction of our poor Huskies. Describe, if you could, the pass to Stutzel which set up the first goal of the game." The video taken from period one began to roll on NESN's screen.

"Well, it worked out well for us. I took a vicious hit by Anderson, at least I think it was, but maintained control and passed it to Mikey who was in perfect position." I assumed the monitors were diagramming the play. "I'm not going to lie to you though, that hit is sure to leave a bruise. Anderson is a heck of a player."

"The third line accounted for four of the ten goals tonight with Stutzel scoring two, then Walsh and DeSchriver adding one a piece while you were on shift. Amazingly, the three forwards on the line are all first year players. How have you three been so successful?"

"It must be the Gatorade." Ugh, why did I say that? "No seriously, Alex, Stutz, and I have been working together since the first practice. We have the ability to know where the other two are at all times and although we don't exhibit a lot of finesse, we're hard-nosed players that get the job done."

"Makes sense. Michigan travels to the campus of Boston University to square off against the Terriers Saturday and Sunday night. However tonight, the Wolverines come to Matthews Arena and dominate the Huskies in a nine-goal victory. Thanks for chatting with us Dave and good luck the rest of the year."

"Thanks a lot."

I wondered how many annoyed viewers in the Massachusetts area just watched 'The Calvetto Conference'. Probably more than I had hoped.

Being the last off the ice, I walked down the tunnel and headed down the hallway for the visitor's locker room. The second I pushed open the door, noise and laughter exploded out from the winning team. The whole area smelled horrendous; full of sweat-drenched pads, jerseys, helmets, undershirts, socks and worst of all, bodies. The steam from the showers sat like a mist at the ceiling of the decrepit room. Luckily, I was getting accustomed to the nauseous atmosphere.

I undressed as teammates, Sean and Alex, asked questions (and poked fun) regarding my interview. Overall, it went fine, but I wasn't too concerned, being an out-of-town station. They could laugh at me all they wanted.

My body had escaped the night's contest with only two bruises; one up around my right shoulder blade and the other on my thigh, the size of a half-dollar. Ed Blackwell would eventually look at my thigh discoloration, but everything would check out fine. Looking at Sean, he wore bumps, bruises and cuts all over his upper half. I never *did* envy the defensemen.

As I wrapped a white towel around my naked waist (ready to start for the row of showers), Trodeau's booming voice filled the locker room.

"Be on the bus at eleven sharp! Eleven o'clock everyone!"

I would have forty minutes to shower, get changed, pack my bag and haul it back to the Michigan-based motor vehicle.

*****

By half past twelve, I was underneath the covers in the hotel bed. Sleeping (or lack thereof) on a bus the previous night, I was thankful for having a cozy resting place. Our team was stationed on the 4th floor of the Ramada Inn and would remain there for three nights, having to drive through the night back to the Lakes State, following the final BU game. I was randomly paired with Scott Hooden in 421, who also enjoyed hitting the hay early. It *was* a bit nerve-racking rooming with our spiritual team leader. Fortunately for me, Scott was very easy-going and we got along well.

The television volume was turned low as I watched the nightly Sportscenter program. No highlights of our game were shown (not surprising for college hockey), but the final score made the ticker at the bottom of the screen. It was pretty incredible too, knowing that I contributed to the score. No, it wasn't the first time and definitely wasn't my pinnacle for the season, however I still got that feeling that our team, my team, was known nationally. Perhaps the viewing public has never heard of a David Calvetto—they aren't familiarized with my rookie-leading six goals and ten assists. They *do*, however, know about the Michigan Wolverine hockey team, being one of the most storied franchises in the sport.

"Hey Dave, do you mind if I shut the TV off?" asked Scott from the next bed. "I'm exhausted."

"Go ahead, I'm not watching it."

With the lights already off, Scott flicked the power switch on the remote control, sending the room into complete darkness. I crawled underneath the sheets and closed my eyes until five minutes later, when they would pop open again.

BANG! BANG! BANG! BANG! I shot up to the infernal pounding on our room's door. Scott merely tossed around in bed and ignored the racket. It sounded as if a mob was rioting outside the walls of room 421.

In a t-shirt and boxers, I staggered, half-asleep, to the door. *It must be the damn hotel security.* I thought. *What could they possibly want at this hour?* To my surprise, it wasn't them at all.

The door swung open and there stood Gerry Walsh, with more of our guys scrambling around behind him.

"Chicks, dude! Chicks!" yelled the senior captain, disregarding the folks trying to sleep.

"What?" I had no idea what was going on. All my eyes showed was a very blurry man in a needlessly bright hallway.

"Chicks! Sixth floor!"

I wore a disgusted look on my face. "What's your point?"

"There's a girl's volleyball team from New York on the sixth floor," said Walsh, finally calming his voice and making some sense. "They invited us up to one of their rooms. They have booze, dude. Booze!"

I just stared at him while squinting.

"What's up with Scott?" asked Gerry.

"He's sleeping."

"What a wimp! So are you coming or not dude?" I thought I'd have to punch him if the word 'dude' left his mouth again. This was easily the most ridiculous conversation I'd ever had. "Well, are you coming or not?"

To this day, I am still unsure why I failed to say 'no' on the spot. Hooden stayed in his bed and I was getting plenty comfortable in mine until the interruption occurred. I badly wanted to resume my slumber.

"Ugh. Hang on, let me throw on some clothes."

"'Atta boy! I wasn't going to take 'no' for an answer so you made the right choice."

"Gee thanks." Leaving Gerry at the door, I went into the small hotel bathroom and splashed some cold water on my face. Refreshing. I made sure to wet my long hair as well and painfully ran a comb through the thick bush.

"Come on slowpoke, let's go!" They're waiting for us!"

"All right, give me a second!" I slipped a pair of gray sweatpants over my boxer shorts and threw on a blue UM hockey sweatshirt, oversized of course, which happened to be unpacked. The sneakers were left underneath the bed, as I would trot upstairs in my white crew socks. As glamorous as it may seem, being a first-year player certainly had its downfalls; it much resembled pledging for a fraternity in the fact that pledges had no say in anything, and all the difficult jobs were unfortunately, yours. How much did I not want to meet these 'chicks'? How much of a choice was I given?

"OK. Let's go," I grunted.

Gerry and I rounded up Derek, Alex, Sean, Eric, Janni (Perner; pronounced Per-nay) and Ben to quietly tiptoe down the hall towards the elevators. The coach along with his colleagues occupied the three connecting rooms in the center of the 4th floor; 416, 418 and 420. We nearly crawled past their doors on all fours, laughing, to avoid a catastrophe. Imagine if our coach caught eight guys sneaking upstairs at 12:30 in the morning. What would we say? "We're just going for ice?"

The elevator made a loud "BING!" as it reached our floor.

"Shhhhhhh!" spoke Eric (Lessard) to the machine.

The nine of us crammed into one elevator and as soon as the doors parted on floor six, we heard the giggling girls.

"Guys!" whispered a tall girl at high volume without her voice cracking. "In here!" She was peering out one of the doors, apparently waiting for us to arrive.

We flocked into the room, led by Captain Gerry, where seven college-age 'chicks' stood, making an incredible clamor.

"Hi guys!" they all seemed to say in unison.

We found out they were the volleyball team from Syracuse University on a weekend trip to play in-conference rival Boston College. The girls were seven of the most sporty and outgoing that I've ever come in contact with, treating us like good friends. Don't ask me how, but they smuggled about four tons of alcohol into the room. If our guys ever got caught with that, we'd be running drills for thirteen straight hours. Easy. We had very strict rules (and morals).

Anyway, it seemed as if the ladies from New York had downed a good portion of the booze by the time our elite eight had arrived. Thumping bass music played loudly on a portable stereo, with most of the girls vivaciously dancing to it. I'll try to quickly describe the seven:

I guessed that none exceeded one hundred and twenty pounds, amazingly (nobody on our hockey team was below one-fifty). Three of the seven girls had blonde hair; another three with brown and the last sported a dyed jet-black style. One of the females was incredibly tall, maybe about six-foot-three (that which welcomed us), with the others a bit shorter than I—maybe between 5'3" and 5'5". The whole bunch wore pajama bottoms and either tees or sweats on top, depending on their body temperature. All but one of the girls, an attractive dark-skinned female who could have been American for all I knew, were Caucasian. Oh yes, and all seven were sloshed—in a Ramada Inn hotel room, no less.

We didn't quite know what to make of the situation until we were properly introduced.

"Hi, I'm Stephanie."

"I'm Tanya."

"Hey, my name is Valerie," they spoke to Sean, Alex, Derek and myself, separated from the rest. "You guys are from Michigan? That's so cool! We're from Syracuse...umm, what state do we live in? New York! That's right, New York! Is it really cold up there in Michigan? Because it snows like crazy in Syracuse! We all hate the snow and the cold! Hey, we have plenty of alcohol, let's all go take a sot...I mean shot."

And so, our drunken night began. Figuring I would only stay for a short time, the team partied long into the night (or should I say morning?). Sean and I toasted to a heavy number of tequila shots, along with whatever other liquor happened to be on the dresser-turned-counter. There was no hiding that I was a lightweight. After a few glasses were stored in my stomach, my memory became a bit fuzzy. I tried to prevent dim-witted words from blurting out of my mouth, but that was nearly hopeless as I remember cackling wildly and dancing around like a fool with the ladies.

"We won tonight!" I recalled yelling to the raucous response of my teammates.

"Northeastern sucks!"

"Northeastern sucks!" chanted everyone. More pointless noise.

Although my memory was blurred from two o'clock on, I did remember a one, Tanya Aiken. Oh, how I wish I never had to mention that name again. She was the lone dark-skinned girl whom I spent most of the night conversing with. To make a long story short, as the blitzed team tiptoed back to the hotel elevators, I decided to follow Tanya to her assigned room down the hall. I didn't actually vividly recall this, but I'm sure it must have happened similarly. From that point forward, the world went black until three hours later.

My eyes slowly unlocked to the sunlight peering through the window curtain. I looked down, confused, head pounding, as my arms, chest and stomach were completely exposed; my UM sweatshirt nowhere to be found. Scott Hooden was not lying in the bed beside mine—in fact, I wasn't alone on my side of the room. Huddled up against my body, bare arm draped across, was a softly snoring Tanya Aiken. My eyes now burst open as my heart pounded a thousand beats per second. Her brown, curly hair lay like a rat's nest below her unclothed shoulders. I slowly lifted the blanket, which we slept under, to see her top half, like mine, was naked to the navel.

How could this have happened? What was I thinking? What have I done?

8

I'll spare you the awkward details of the next couple minutes. All you need to know is that I escaped, as quickly as possible, in one piece. I *did* awake the sleeping Tanya and couldn't elude the customary kiss goodbye. Millions of thoughts crossed my mind while I found my clothes and blasted out the door; should I feel upset regarding the mind-destructed evening or should I be delighted, considering an attractive girl took me to her hotel room? And it was right about then when the worst possible thought that could cross my mind, did indeed, cross my mind. A thought that took my legs out from under me, nearly making me collapse. A thought that felt as if my heart leaped from my insides. A thought that formed sweat upon my forehead and trickled all the way down to the ends of my toes. A thought that would never again feel the same. At that early morning moment, I thought of my girlfriend, Amy.

Luckily, a sudden distraction caused me to focus elsewhere. Looking down the sixth floor hallway, I spotted my friend Sean, out cold on the carpet. He rested on his bulk stomach with head upon his outstretched arm and a large puddle of drool on the floor beside it.

"Sean!" I called to him in a loud whisper. No answer. "Sean!"

Realizing that we'd be busted before long, I went to wake up my buddy.

"Ugh," grunted Sean as I tapped his shoulder numerous times. "What time is it?"

"It's six-forty five, man. Come on, we have to get back to our rooms."

The large Sean Collins propped his head up. "Where the hell am I?"

"I'll try to explain later. We have fifteen minutes before wakeup call and if Trodeau catches us up here, we're dead."

Sean, appearing to be in as much pain as I, stumbled to his feet and followed me to the elevators. There was no activity on the 6th floor while we waited for the winch to bring us two stories down. No sign of the Syracuse women's volleyball team could be seen—and for me, that was a good thing.

Sean and I began to chat when we stepped into the opening elevator.

"What happened to you last night?" questioned my teammate while digging fingers into his aching forehead.

"I have absolutely no idea."

"I remember you leaving with that dark-skinned girl at some point. Did you stay in her room?"

"I stayed in her bed."

"With her in it?"

"Yep."

"Dude!" yelled Sean, grinning from ear to ear. "Did you guys…you know…"

"I have no idea."

"You don't remember if you slept together?"

"Nope."

"Not at all?"

"Nope."

"No?"

"Nope."

"Wow!" remarked Sean. "You must have been out of it. I must say, you were hilarious last night."

"Yeah?"

"Yeah."

The elevator beeped and halted at the fourth floor, temporary home to our hockey team. As the doors parted, Sean and I took two steps forward and immediately froze solid. My morning had rapidly gotten worse.

Lined up against the hallway wall were all our teammates along with the entire coaching staff pacing before them. At that second, I wished to be invisible. Maybe if I did an about-face and closed myself inside the elevator, nobody would notice. Unfortunately, my plea was too late as the whole group turned in our direction. We were busted.

"Ah, here's the last two," stated Jerry Trodeau with a cynical smile. "We were beginning to worry about you guys." Sean and I had panic-stricken looks upon our hung-over faces. "Well, now that we're all accounted for, you can all go back to your rooms. Breakfast is at eight on the first floor. After breakfast, about eight forty five or so, I expect everyone involved in last night's fiasco to meet me outside at the hotel entrance. If you were involved and don't show up then believe me, I will find out and you will never play another game for Michigan." Another cynical expression. "Understand? Well, all right then. Jeff, Ed, Rich, Red; anything to add?"

"For everyone else who wasn't involved, be at the buses at nine-thirty. We leave at quarter of."

Before I was even fully awake, with head throbbing, deep trouble had found me. I was stuck in a horrible predicament. The last few months had been some of the best in my life, playing for the yellow and blue; and to think that my future with the team was in jeopardy mesmerized me. All due to one night, one decision, one girl.

The most I could do was ignore the fact while in the shower and attempting to eat the hotel's continental breakfast. My appetite was non-existent that morning. Just looking at the sesame seed bagel on the plate before me made my stomach churn over and over and over again. The team chowed down like normal, not bothered by their ruthless hangovers. They acted as if nothing occurred mere hours ago.

Judgment time had come as the guilty party sauntered through the lobby and out the revolving door to the hotel's main entrance. All those involved were present, including Sean and I, who, quite possibly, would receive the heaviest blows. We all wore solemn faces, that is, all except, Gerry Walsh, who was all smiles and snickers from some reason or another. It was then that it pretty much hit me; Gerry thrived on getting rookies in trouble. He basically forced me out of bed and probably did the same to Alex and Derek (I imagine Sean voluntarily tagged along as I guessed he could crush the captain).

Our coach, along with assistant Ridley, angrily joined us in the frigid outdoors, not speaking a single word for what seemed like hours. We stood there, waiting for the dragon to spew its fire.

"So!" finally exclaimed the fiery beast. "Anything to say?" Silence. "That's funny, it seems as if you couldn't say enough last night. The hotel security came to our door early this morning to notify Jeff and I of your wrongdoings. You woke up half the damn hotel!" Jerry's voice was consistently rising. "We are one of the classiest franchises in the sport and now I have to basically beg the manager to stay here for two more nights. You guys completely embarrassed all of us! So talk, what do you have to say?"

Gerry was the first to speak up. "Well, there was a girl's volleyball team from—"

"I don't give a damn!" butted in the coach. "This regards you! Not them!"

Coach Ridley was next to add a few words. "Do you guys even realize how difficult it is to book fourteen rooms for a hockey team? We could easily be sleeping on some high school's gym floor, but we did this for you. And now, you had to go and ruin it."

"Coach," tried Walsh again. "It was the girls that had—"

"Shut up Gerry! As the captain of this team, I expect *you*, most of all, to fess up to your mistakes!"

"Sorry Coach." Finally, the lips of o' captain, my captain zipped.

"All right." Trodeau sighed loudly."Obviously, I can't suspend all eight of you or we'd have to start forfeiting games—which is *not* an option. So, that's the dilemma Jeff and I faced during breakfast, what to do?

"We've come up with a pretty fair solution to the mess. *If* the hotel's manager will let us stay, you will all be locked down as soon as we return the next two nights. As for today, you will run extra drills and during dinner, you guys will stay with me at the practice facility to watch game video. Does that sound fair?"

We nodded our heads in agreement. Sounded fair.

"Good. We leave in twenty minutes, go grab everything you need for today. Collins and Calvetto, stay here, I want to speak with you two."

We knew it was too good to be true. Trodeau was about to lay the hammer down on us both.

The coach wasted no time in getting to the point. "You two are suspended for one game. Tomorrow night, bring a shirt and tie to the arena and you'll sit at the end of the bench with us (the skipper always ordered us to bring one dressy shirt, tie and a pair of khaki pants wherever we traveled). Do either of you want to oppose this?"

I was raring to tell Coach Trodeau about jackass Gerry Walsh and his policy of not taking 'no' for an answer. I was forced into this predicament and I sincerely hoped our captain would pay the price.

"No sir," I answered. "That's fair." And that was the correct response. If I brought Gerry down with me, not only would we be at fighting terms, but our team would suffer as well. It just wasn't worth it.

Sean nodded his head at the wise coach. "It's fair. We're really sorry about the mess."

"Alright, I'm done with you. Go upstairs and get all your stuff. I'll see you two on the bus."

*****

Friday was an excruciating morning and afternoon for the eight men accused. We ran skating, shooting, offensive, defensive, passing, checking, power play, penalty kill, face-off, 3-man drills, and every other play book formation under the sun all day, numbing my legs for a good while.The other seven also seemed fatigued by dinnertime (game video time for us).

The evening was spent touring Boston, as my party-friendly group was lucky to attend. We visited the famed Boston Common, Granary Burying Ground (home to John Hancock, Adams and others), the Italian North End and even got the privilege of going to the Fleetcenter for a Boston Bruins game. No, it wasn't our beloved Red Wings but we still had a great time sitting in the upper balcony. The giant scoreboard even welcomed us to the cheer of the crowd.

Saturday, it was right back to work. After a night of being locked down, I was well rested for a change. Our team scouted BU from the videos (thanks to us), and ran sufficient drills to prepare. With my legs still sore like lead weights, it actually wasn't terrible to be sitting out of the night's contest. It was still depressing, but not terrible.

As for the match-up with BU, we skated to a 2-2 tie, utilizing primarily three lines with Sean and I sitting out. The coaching staff bumped right-winger, Joseph Vitek, up to the third line and occasionally rotated him out. The guilt occupying my head during the game was unbearable. Knowing I could have assisted the team, I wanted to kick myself for leaving the hotel room on Thursday night. It seemed that when every bad Wolverine play occurred, Trodeau would shoot Sean and I a terrible look as if to say, 'That mistake was YOUR fault.'

The squad was a bit let down after the game; the newer of the two locker rooms being more subdued. We would eventually work out the kinks on Sunday morning and drive back to Walter Brown Arena, where the Terriers awaited us again.

Tonight, returning to my blue hockey jersey once again, I rejoined mates Alex and Mike on the third line. The crowd was lighter than the previous evening due to the winter storm throwing snow around outdoors. *The Syracuse women's volleyball team hated the snow,*

I thought. Inside, the storm was the Terriers, invading the ice like a house on fire.

After Eric Lessard gave our team a 1-0 advantage, BU netted three unassisted goals, all 94 seconds apart. Taking the wind out of our sails, we monotonously skating the final two periods, courteously bowing out to the home team, 4-1.

The CaSH line (Calvetto, Stutzel, Hutchinson) got ruthlessly dominated all night. Our passes were frequently wide and when actually accurate, would skip over a stick, forcing a careless turnover. I recorded two shots on net, both weak and easily gloved by the talented goaltender. Mike and Alex had zero. It was a game we hoped to forget soon as our weekend finished on a discouraging note. The now third-place Wolverines, once again, had only picked up three of a possible six points. I could tell everyone was letdown.

Not until 5 p.m. the following evening, did the team bus arrive back at its home base of Ann Arbor. It was a leg-cramping ride through the night and I had nothing better to do than think (a lot of garbage sat in my mind from the lengthy weekend). With headphones covering my ears, I thought about my suspension; would my teammates view me in a different light now? I relived the events of Thursday night in my mind, from *REM* sleep to a roaring party to lying partially naked beside a total stranger. I lamented on my poor Sunday evening performance in the loss to BU, thinking my play was obviously affected by the highly uncommon weekend. Never before was I so delighted to return to my home state—I couldn't wait to put the Boston trip behind me and continue with my normal, subdued life.

Many girlfriends met my teammates as the bus pulled into the Yost parking lot. I wished I had somebody in the lot but I knew there was a beautiful girl in Ohio awaiting a phone call. I wasted no time in dialing her number back at the dormitory.

*****

December sixth felt like a typical northern winter's day. Snow flurries fell upon the campus pond and ice began to form at its edges.

The ground was a bright white shade with footprints here and there from the stampeding students. The sky loomed around the University in a dull gray color. It was a tone of gray that almost slipped the cheery into gloominess, the outspoken into silence, the proper into the slouched, the fat into the freezing.

I spent the precious few minutes between classes on my favorite wooden bench, sketching the wintry scene. My entire green, one-subject notebook was dedicated to drawings of this and that dating back to my final year of high school. Today's doodle wasn't my best effort by any means (for one, it was just too damn cold). Snowflakes would land on my paper and moisten the surface, making it impossible to avoid the smudge. Oh well. I was just killing time anyway.

The regular couples that usually occupied the lawn had thinned out. Only one boyfriend / girlfriend pair sat cuddling for warmth on one of the benches across from mine. Not surprisingly, the two brought Amy to mind and unfortunately, it wasn't all happy and gay thoughts. To tell you the truth, I was a bit annoyed with my longtime girlfriend. The telephone call on Monday night was a sour one as I assumed Ms. Lewis was in a rotten mood. She consistently commented on my tone of voice and how I just didn't seem like myself. So who was I, then? My tone of voice was the same as ever. I said "I love you" and "I miss you" during the phone call, but for some reason, she didn't completely believe me. Whatever. No big deal; she'll shake it off.

1:33. It was seven minutes until my European history class and knowing me, I would wait until the last possible minute to attend. Being an enormous lecture hall, the professor didn't know me from the next guy so strolling in tardy wasn't a major problem.

No Frisbee games occurred today in the grassy (now snowy) knoll. No studying, reading or writing was done outdoors. It was just I, bundled in my winter parka, notebook perched on my legs, and the cold couple on the adjacent bench. Three more weeks and the Christmas holiday would be upon us.

*****

The week of December 5th through the 9th was a rather boring one for the team and I, as no games took place and practices were cancelled for three days, giving us a much-needed break. Believe it or not, we actually had to attend all our week's classes, something we weren't accustomed to. Finals Week was scheduled from Monday the 19th through Thursday and our strategically planned schedule only allowed us one game from the present day until the month-long Christmas break. Most other colleges operated in the same fashion—they believed in the whole junk regarding academics over athletics. I have to tell you though, I spent more time studying after the Boston weekend than I had all semester. Hockey occupies a lot of time.

Students had begun to acknowledge me around campus, knowing my name and face from the games. Those who didn't attend the weekend matches could read about us in the daily campus newspaper, as frequently, photos of the team would be printed. Even those that didn't follow the sport knew most of our names from word of mouth. Occasionally, I would receive a 'Hi Dave' from a passing student or teacher. It was definitely an abnormal feeling, being the talk of the town, but I rather enjoyed it. Never before had I felt like a true celebrity.

In our final match prior to the holiday break, the team returned to our winning ways, defeating Ferris State, 4-0. With the victory, we returned to the second spot, past the slumping Michigan State Spartans. The Christmas standings were as follows:

Ohio St.	34 pts
Michigan.	28 pts
Michigan St.	27 pts
Lake Superior	23 pts
Alaska-Fairbanks	20 pts
Notre Dame	20 pts
Bowling Green	15 pts
Northern Michigan	15 pts
Western Michigan	15 pts

Nebraska-Omaha	12 pts
Miami (Ohio)	11 pts
Ferris St.	7 pts

Lake Superior St. came into the break hot, riding a season-high five game winning streak that powered them into fourth place. Our rival, Ohio State, was unexcitedly playing .500 hockey while Ferris State had tumbled to the bottom of the barrel, losing seven of their last eight.

After the Ferris game on the 16th, college hockey was suspended until January the fifth. This lull gave us a chance to focus on our final examinations and spend Christmas / Chanukah / Kwanza / Ramadan and the New Year with our families. Unfortunately, the long break often caused dust to form on the team playbooks. The school would set up temporary housing for us through the holiday break as most of our permanent dormitories were locked up for safety's sake. But I'll discuss that further when the time comes. I often have a tendency to get ahead of myself.

My mother assisted me in the process of vacating my dorm room on the morning of December 21st. All students were to remove their valuables prior to the break, which for me, was nearly everything in the room. The two of us lugged the computer, television, VCR, stereo, futon, boxes and trunks to the car on that absolutely frigid Wednesday morning and drove the forty miles back to Fenton. I hadn't realized until then that Thanksgiving weekend was the last time I'd been home—nearly a month ago. The place still looked the same; downstairs spic and span, Mikey's room a landfill site and my bedroom an empty wasteland, deserted from all the electronics and appliances taken to college. Tables, couches and chairs from the first floor sat in their usual positions. (It wasn't like I expected the place to appear differently, but in a way, I hoped it would).

Fenton, Michigan was also the same as I had left it. The business' and restaurants remained operational, the schools functional and the thousands of single-family homes were in tact. It takes a lot for a town to alter its appearance, especially when it's your hometown. Places that fall out of business and new companies taking their spot often caused the biggest stir. "This weekend only, come to Best Buy's grand opening sale in Fenton! Get name brand merchandise at half the sticker price! Sony, Aiwa, RCA, Toshiba, Bose, Olympus, its all here! So come on down to Best Buy, route thirty-eight, Fenton." That was about the only way to lure people into our municipality. And let me tell you, an event of that magnitude drove our townsfolk into frenzy. Needless to say, we had a dull city.

On the corner of Hampton and Riendeau stood the familiar favorite, Guiseppi's, an Italian pizzeria and sub shop. I worked as a cook (if you can even call it that) for the past two summers, making pizzas and sandwiches in the back room with my boss and shop owner, Steven Toscano. All of his employees were full-blooded Italian descendants, making us popular amongst most of the customers. The shop was a small, cozy one with ten or eleven red, high-top tables set up around the sidewalls. On Friday and Saturday evenings, every one of them, without fail, would be occupied.

During that freezing Wednesday afternoon, after unloading my car, I worked up an appetite and ran down to Guiseppi's for a bite to eat. The crew couldn't have been happier to see me.

"Davie! How you doing?" echoed Steven's voice through the smoke and sizzles of the back room. "We were wondering if you would come by!"

One of the four order-taking girls, a cute seventeen-year-old high school senior, who was on shift, said her hellos. "Did you come by to help us out?"

"No, I'm just getting something to eat."

"Well, you know where everything is."

With that, I was granted permission into the back, slipped on an apron and threw a handful of steak on the steaming fryer. I couldn't argue with free food (even if I *did* have to make it myself).

Owner Steven Toscano was in his usual cheery afternoon mood. He flipped the meat with exhilaration off the large fryer while whistling a tune at the same time. Occasionally, he'd sing as well.

"So Davie my boy, how school treating you?" said my former boss in that cute Italian enunciation.

"Good, good. Our hockey team is playing quite well."

"Eyy! Very good! My wife and I watch de game on television a few weeks back. I still not fully understand de game of ice hockey. Very confusing to me."

"Well, you should come to a game this year. Being able to see it in person certainly helps you grasp the concept." I began to dice the steak into fine pieces.

"Yes, I try to make it. But with de shop and all, I don't know. Very busy."

"How are things going here anyway?"

The smile vanished from Steve's face. "Oh, not so good. You remember dat cook I hired before you leave for school?"

"Yeah, Phil?" I questioned.

"Yes, yes. He just quit de other day. Didn't show up for work, no call either. Finally, he come in near closing and turn in his apron. No explanation." Steve shook his head. "Unbelievable."

"That's too bad," I answered the 47-year-old Italian. "I'm sure you'll find somebody to fill his spot."

"That's de problem Davie, I can't get work." A light bulb suddenly, clicked on in Steven Toscano's head. "Davie! Can you work for us during your break?"

I saw that coming from eight miles away. "I don't know Mr. Toscano, I've been pretty busy with—"

"I pay you under de table. Sixty dollar a night."

"I don't think I'll be able to—"

"Seventy dollar, eighty! You can come in at four and work 'till close. Please Davie, you my best employee. De place isn't de same without you."

The store telephone rang as the seventeen-year-old Meghan jotted down a customer's order. The cash register *cha-chinged* open; a sound all too familiar to me. I was trapped.

"I can only work for two weeks because our season starts back up on the sixth."

"Yes, yes! Dat will give me time to find work!" Thank you Davie! I promise I pay you real good!"

Feeling like a hand puppet whose strings were being toyed with, I sliced open a roll and tossed my hot sandwich meat inside. Mr. Toscano always had his way of convincing. Luckily, he was a good person to work for (which was the lone reason for accepting his offer, I convinced myself). Oh yeah, and the other reason; more free food.

I began my winter work at the peak hours of that night, grinding out orders with my new appreciative buddy, Mr. Toscano. It wasn't as terrible as I had originally assumed, especially since I had plenty of spare time, the first of which dating back to September. Don't ask me why, but the place was very crowded around the holiday. Who wants to order out for pizzas and hoagies on the Christmas weekend? Strange!

Within forty-eight hours of being back in Fenton, my bedroom looked similar to it's past summer's appearance; it gave me that classic 'home sweet home' feel. The outside of our house was decked with Christmas lights, clear and colored, with a single candle in each window. Our year's Christmas tree sat in the living room, top branch touching the ceiling. A handful of wrapped presents sat beneath the huge pine from distant relatives and even some labeled from Mom and Dad. Mikey and I had grown out of the Santa Claus phase—actually, it was years ago when we found out, but the folks continued to humor us.

Anyway, I won't bore you anymore with the 'holiday season' mumbo-jumbo. I was pretty fatigued when the 25th arrived from working four straight evenings at Guiseppi's while still exhausted from finals week. Christmas Day would hopefully serve as a nice break.

9

Loving Father,
help us remember the birth of Jesus,
that we may share in the song of the angels,
the gladness of the shepherds,
and the worship of the wise men.

Close the door of hate
and open the door of love all over the world.
Let kindness come with every gift
and good desires with every greeting.
Deliver us from evil by the blessing
which Christ brings,
and teach us to be merry with clear hearts.
May the Christmas morning
make us happy to be thy children
and Christmas evening bring us to our beds
with grateful thoughts,
forgiving and forgiven, for Jesus' sake.
Amen.

—Robert Louis Stevenson

The holiday was spent, as normal, up in Palms Point with the usual cast of characters. It was nothing special; nothing memorable and certainly, nothing like Christmas' of old. Did you ever notice how the holidays tend to be more humdrum and meaningless as time moves on? We all remember the days as a young child; rising at the crack of dawn to run down the stairs and tear into the vast mountain of presents. Those events would diminish just slightly every year, until you almost wished to remain in bed. Turning twenty years old, I probably spent more money on my parents, girlfriend, brother, relatives and friends combined, than I received. But hey, 'tis the season of giving is what they say. I would soon be thankful for the paychecks at Guiseppi's.

The actual afternoon of the 25th read upwards of fifty degrees on the thermometers with not a trace of snow around. Unseasonably warm weather. It felt like Christmas in Bermuda, minus the beautiful scenery. Normally, a Michigan Christmas called for blizzard conditions with maybe some gale-force winds thrown in for excitement.

When we departed the ranch house long after dinner, I met up with Amy on her side of town. I agreed to take an evening jog with her, down her normal three-mile route, which zigzagged across East

Fenton. All the streets were well lit, making it perfectly safe to be outdoors after dark. We would observe the decorative holiday lights on all the houses along the way.

As I said, the weather was unseasonably warm so the wind didn't numb our exposed faces. Amy, running track for upwards of six years now, was accustomed to jogging in the cold. I, however, was not. Hockey didn't exactly require a great deal of running, although much of the team did practice this in their free time to remain in peak physical condition. I didn't.

As we scampered through the sidewalks of Fenton, I became winded much quicker than my girlfriend. I huffed and puffed, my face redder than hell while Amy jogged at full throttle about twenty feet ahead.

"Hey!" I yelled, breathing heavily. "Wait for me!"

Amy stopped momentarily. "Come on, hurry up!"

"Sorry…babe. You're…better at this…than…I am."

I halted to catch my breath in front of an unpaved driveway. I guess it had been longer than I thought since I jogged with my physically fit significant other. I figured the hockey nearly every day would help me out. Guess that's a whole different animal.

After a few seconds rest, the two of us continued to trot down the lighted side streets, but within a short period of time, Amy was once again running far ahead of me.

"Babe! Don't you want to…talk with me…while you run?"

Amy turned and backpedaled, seeming very impatient with me. "You're too slow," she complained.

"I…don't run track."

"Maybe you should."

I was a bit taken back as Amy had never before spoken to me in this tone. I stopped once again to catch my breath.

"Is something wrong?"

"No."

"It seems like you're bothered by something."

"No, nothing's wrong. Come on, let's go." She put her feet in motion and glided down the sidewalk once again.

"Of course," I muttered to myself. This girl was going to make me collapse and die. I can't believe that I used to be able to keep up with her. Those Bowling Green track stars must run a mile a minute.

I no longer attempted to catch up with my speedy girlfriend. Staggering far behind, I breathed in the cool air while trying to figure out what species of bug had crawled up Amy's butt. She *did* tell me that she detested holidays with her family. Maybe the afternoon had taken its toll on her, forcing her into an unpleasant mood. I decided to leave her alone until she snapped to.

After another quarter mile where Amy scooted along ahead of me, her legs finally slowed down.

"Phew." I wiped the sweat from my forehead. Amy came to an abrupt halt, her facial makeup smeared around her eyes and a black tear rolling off her cheek. "Is the wind making your eyes water?"

No answer. Instead, my girlfriend turned her head away and covered it with her cupped hands. Drops of water fell to the pavement beneath her.

"Hun?"

Still no answer. Now, sobbing noises could be heard as I quickly became concerned.

"Amy, what's the matter? Was your day really *that* bad?"

Between sobs, my girlfriend said to me, "You just don't get it, Dave."

"What? What don't I get? Amy, what don't I get?" For drama, it took her quite some time to respond.

Ms. Lewis removed her two hands from the facial area, revealing her tear-infested cheeks with mascara now running down the sides of her nose. My heart skipped a couple beats before it sank to my stomach as I looked at my crying girlfriend. After ten uncomfortable seconds, she finally decided to speak.

"You *have* changed David. As much as you refuse to admit it, it's true."

"What are you talking about babe?"

"Don't call me that," Amy immediately responded with a snap.

"I've been calling you that for two years!"

"Well, I don't like it. And I don't like who you've become."

"Who have I become!"

"I don't know." The tears flowed like a river, splashing to the ground. I stood confused. "I don't know," Amy repeated. "You're not the David Calvetto I fell in love with—things just aren't the same between us. I can't go on much longer feeling depressed every day." The dam collapsed and water gushed out uncontrollably. "I just can't do it."

Words cannot even begin to describe the thoughts and feelings occupying my mind at that particular point in time. I couldn't decide whether to be angry, heartbroken, or just plain confused. In a way, I was all three. *Did she know?* I wondered. *How could she know? It's impossible!*

"Amy," I started by saying. "What in the hell is going on here? Why didn't you tell me any of this before?"

"You didn't want to listen."

"Of course I did! Why would I want it to come to this?"

"I've tried talking for the past month but you've consistently changed the subject. I can't deal with it anymore!"

"Okay fine, let's talk!" I exclaimed, attempting to solve the problem. "We can fix this problem now, I'm ready to talk."

"David, it's too late," I understood between Amy's blubbers. "It can't be fixed. Maybe we can talk about this somewhere down the line...but not today." Opting not to speak again, Amy began to jog away from a stupefied me, tears rolling down her face, onto her already damp shirtsleeve. I watched in disbelief as the love of my life scampered down the street, not once looking back.

"Amy!" I called out in hopes that she would stop dead and come running back to me, arms held open (like the famous movie scene amidst the field of flowers). However, on this Christmas night, I had no such luck.

Just as suddenly as our relationship had begun that summer's night on the cool beach sand, it had ended nearly two and a half years later. I remained standing in the same position minutes after Amy had fallen out of sight. More than likely, I failed to move a muscle either. Being confused was one thing, but what had just occurred was completely another. My whole body tingled. My feet were numb. My head was a two-ton slab of rock, caving in from it's own weight. I had been dumped. Dumped by the only girl I had ever loved.

This was certainly a Christmas I've never forgotten, but for all the wrong reasons. My parents would later question why I was home so early but I would shrug them off and climb up to my bedroom, closing and locking the door behind me. My kid brother was out, spending the holiday evening with his high school chums while I lay on my bed, huddled underneath the blankets, watching rerun episodes of Three's Company. Merry Christmas.

*****

Amy Lewis and I reclined in the two front seats of her brand new Ford Escort (a used vehicle, but new to the first-year driver) while gazing up into the night's sky. The red automobile was parked in our favorite getaway spot; a secluded beach located twelve miles north of Detroit that we frequently traveled to on sunny weekends. Imagine the most picturesque spot visited and multiply that by three. The water was forever crystal clear and yachts recurrently roamed the beautiful harbor piloted by the friendliest people this side of Michigan. Some day, the two of us wised to own one of these boats—the S.S. Lewis perhaps. All four windows to the Escort were rolled down as the pair of us soaked in the cool summer's breeze. The date was July of 2001.

Following our short barefoot jaunt along the sand, my girlfriend and I talked up a storm in the parked car.

"What am I going to do without you next year, Dave?" Amy inquired as she rolled on her side to look at me.

Without me? What am I going to do without you? Thinking of the coming situation made us weepy (internally of course). Could we survive a long-distance relationship?

"I'm sure we can survive a long-distance relationship." Okay, that answered my question. Amy heavily sighed and followed up by saying, "I'm just going to miss you."

"Well, we'll still be able to spend weekends together—I'll have no reason to stay at school. I could come to your place, or you could come to Ann Arbor—or even home so we can still drive here." Amy's face lit up. I leaned across the stick shift for a kiss and whispered closely, "I love you."

Ms. Lewis grew giddy. "I love you too…let's make a pact."

"Which would be—?"

"Let's never break up with each other," she spoke half-humouredly, revealing both dimples. "I couldn't live without you."

The comment made me titter. "Alright honey…sounds good to me."

*****

New Year's Eve came and no word was received from my recent ex. I called her house and cellular phone a combination of roughly fifteen times to no response as I guess she wasn't 'ready to talk' yet. Due to this, the six days between Christmas and the 31st of December were some of the toughest I have ever lived. I worked every night with Steven and the girls at Guiseppi's while despising every minute of it. I screwed up orders left and right and uncommonly used foul language in the back room as well as in front of customers. Mr. Toscano was probably second-guessing himself for re-hiring me.

I didn't discuss the breakup with anyone; not my parents, not my brother, not my hometown friends, not my co-workers; nobody. The only people I'd consider spilling my heart out to were surprisingly, Sean Collins, Michael Stutzel and Alex Hutchinson but unfortunately, we were separated due to the school break. As far as my family was concerned, Amy and I were together and well. After work, I would drive around town for an hour, mellowing out by listening to music, while I would tell my mother I was over my girlfriend's house. She didn't need to know quite yet, and for that matter, neither did Mikey, who I'm sure wouldn't improve the situation. I had to remain superior to my younger brother. Besides, I was positive that once January fifth rolled around and I was back at Ann Arbor with the boys, everything would be fine. The situation just pained me at the present moment.

At seven o'clock on the eve of the New Year, Mikey was already out with his friends while my folks celebrated with the rest of Fenton's finest at the downtown American Legion. Meanwhile, I remained by myself at home. It had been numerous years since I could recall a New Year's Eve as boring and forlorn as this one. I spent the front part of the evening lounging around and lamenting, eating a bowl of popcorn in my sweatpants at one point while channel surfing through college football bowl games. Over and over, I thought, *How could one lousy girl have this kind of effect on me?*

I had nearly dozed off when the house phone rang.

"Hello?"

"Hey, is this Dave?" came the male voice from the other end.

"Yeah. Who's this?"

"It's Kurt! You know, Kurt from high school."

A smile popped on my face. "Kurty! How have you been?"

"Good, good, thanks for asking. Hey, I'm calling because a bunch of us are hanging over my house tonight. If you're not busy, come on by."

"Sounds good," I answered my old friend when I suddenly changed my mind. "I'd love to stop in but I have to meet up with my hockey team soon. We have a function tonight in Detroit, something to do with First Night." Don't ask me how I was making up these vicious lies. "Sorry man, I wish I could come."

"Oh, it's all right. Give me a call sometime. Have fun in the city."

"Thanks. Talk to you later." And I hung up.

You wouldn't completely understand. Even though I didn't want to be alone, I *did* want to be alone. To everyone else, that was probably the wrong decision but to me, it was right. Unfortunately.

I *did* have one more telephone conversation late that evening. It was approximately five minutes to twelve when I dialed Amy's cell, fully expecting to reach her voicemail. I prepared a 'Happy New Year Speech' in my head for her to receive later, but instead, the rings ceased after three and a plethora of loud voices could be heard.

"Hello?" came Amy's voice, ringing above the others.

I panicked. "A-Amy?"

"Yes?" she answered, waiting for a response.

"Hey, it's Dave."

"Yes, I know."

"Oh. Well, um…I'm just calling to say Happy New Year," I managed to spit out.

"Thanks."

"Where are you tonight?"

"Why do you need to know?" she responded with a question (never a good sign).

"Oh, ah…I was just wondering. I can hardly hear you because of the noise."

"Well, I'm out."

"Out where?"

"I'm just out! Okay? That's all you need to know. I don't have any time to talk so I have to go."

"Amy, wait," I pleaded. "At least tell me—"

A dial tone hummed loudly in my ear, sending me into a radical state of frustration. Without thinking, I hurled the cordless telephone across the room, watching it smash into pieces against the far wall. "Goddamnit!"

The television cut live to New York City where thousands of crazy partygoers were counting the seconds to midnight. They lined the streets, packed tightly, as the giant glowing ball could be spotted sliding down the pole. Streamers and balloons were prematurely let loose into the night sky. "The New York time shows eleven fifty-nine, ladies and gentlemen," spoke Dick Clark from a rooftop in Times Square. "It is *pandemonium* here as we are quite possible looking at the biggest New Year's Eve crowd ever assembled. And here we go, the ball has begun is dissent! This is it folks!" Traditionally, this was the most joyous night of the year, signaling 'the new beginning.' For me, it felt like the end.

"Three…two…one…Happy New Year!!"

January 2003

10

"Ladies and gentlemen, please welcome...YOUR two-thousand and three...Michigan Wolverines!"

We paraded out the tunnel and on to our home ice, lead as always by the goalie, Scott Hooden. The usual sound operator played 'Welcome To The Jungle', as during the course of the season, I had learned nearly all the *Guns N' Roses* lyrics. The rock anthem jacked our team up for every home contest.

The twenty of us were especially motivated for this game, the first of the New Year. I had literally counted the days on my calendar to the present date of January sixth. Following a rough semester break (to say the least), I was thankful to return to the university and especially to be on our home ice for this much-awaited match. As soon as I emerged from the tunnel and hit the ice surface, my mind was completely focused on the opponent at hand (non-conference Minnesota was in town tonight). I'm sure I've already mentioned that hockey is my escape from reality. Well, never before was this statement so true than at this very moment; I couldn't wait to erase the holidays from my short-term memory.

The eighteen guys (offense and defensemen) skated in donuts around our net, slapping the pads of the Hoover every time around the crease. We warmed the Hobey Baker candidate up with a few shots until he was ready to go; the customary pre-game routine.

"Go get 'em Scotty!"

Neither immediate family nor friends drove out to Ann Arbor on this chilly evening, which was actually a good thing. The last thing I needed was an unnecessary distraction from the stands to alter my game. I would focus on hockey and *only* hockey for the sixty minutes following the drop of the puck. Come on, let's go.

In a coaching move prior to the game, freshman Joseph Vitek (one of Trodeau's favorites) was bumped up to the second line to skate between Jeff Thomas and junior, Nolan Van Eaves. Jerry elected to switch up the struggling line as we also swapped a few defensive pairings with Collins in the mix. Vitek's new line got the nod at the outset of the game and unfortunately for our star coach, played rather poorly. Joseph simply wasn't yet accustomed to skating beside two upperclassmen, looking quite lost out on the ice. Luckily, our scrappy third line remained healthy and intact and hoped into play for the first time at the 15:22 mark.

It had been two weeks too long since my blades had converged with the wet, cold ice in the heat of battle. Heart pounding, I sped down the right wing, jumping into the offensive zone. The muscular giant, Sean Collins, carried the puck up with his new line mate, Ben O'Conner, while Alex, Stutz and I camped out at the blue line, careful of the offside. Our very dangerous opponent changed up their battalion and attacked us on the defensive end.

"Sean! Up, up!" yelled Alex on the opposite wing from I, signaling for the puck. Collins skipped it off the boards as Hutch dug it out on the fly and carried deep into the zone. Stutz and I were blanketed by defensemen, forcing our left-winger to take an errant shot, sailing far off from the goal. I fought to get behind the net but a Golden Gopher (Minnesota's very gay team name) rode me off the play, sending my body into the right wing corner glass.

"Ohhhhh," moaned the crowd.

In an easy maneuver, number two of the Gophers glided up to the idle puck and slapped it around the boards, sending it out past center ice. The three forwards (me included) followed our standard routine by getting behind the blue line and waiting for the upcoming attack. Sean lazily regrouped the puck in front of our goal and turned up ice.

I made sure to glance at the home team's bench for any gesture from Trodeau, Blemenson or Ridley. Jerry stood behind his players, arms flailing, however the excited coach wasn't my primary focus.

Directly behind the spirited man, on the opposite side of the glass, sat my ex-girlfriend. She held a fountain drink in one hand and was currently pointing something out with the other. This was NOT what I needed. My muscles went numb; sweat trickled from my hairline. I nearly lost the grip on my stick as I now gripped on with both hands. Looking even more closely now, I noticed this person was not Amy Lewis at all, but rather some middle-aged woman, pointing to the scoreboard.

"Get a grip," I mumbled. "You know she's not here."

Shaking my head back into place, I kicked my CCM's in gear.

TWEET! The head ref sounded his whistle, spotting a Wolverine player in the Minnesota zone.

"Offside on fourteen!"

"Damn it!" I began the play before the puck (or any teammates) had crossed the line, pinning the penalty on me. I slumped my head, skating all the way back to the bench in this fashion. I badly wanted to shield myself from the disappointed crowd.

"Callie!" bellowed old man Red. "Pay attention, will you? Come on now!" I deserved that.

Sitting on the bench, awaiting our line's next shift, I spoke to no one. I haphazardly followed the play of the scoreless game while my mind fought large-scaled mêlées with itself. More than once, I wheeled my body around to double, triple and quadruple check that Amy wasn't there. How did she appear to be in attendance only minutes ago? I was convinced that insanity had overtaken me. Or something similar.

The scoreboard read 6:41 and counting in the opening period when Trodeau called for our line at the next stoppage of play. The opening thirteen minutes of the contest lived up to it's billing; hard hitting and a very fast pace up and down the ice. We could out-skate virtually every opponent that stepped into the rink which usually—and could eventually - work to our advantage. Our bevy would never tire.

Michael took the face-off in the Gopher zone, getting wood on the puck first and wristing it at the opposing net minder. Slap. The fans awwwed as the puck ricocheted off the right kneepad of the masked goalkeeper. Routine save. Staying on the play, I winded my stick up for a blazing slap shot, however, I connected with air, nearly corkscrewing me into the ice. The Minnesota forward easily gained control of the puck and raced down the wing. What was going on here?

Luckily, the coaching staff spared me a verbal assault while I skated by the bench area, into our zone. The team dressed in rouge peppered Scott Hooden with wrist shots that were all kicked away, keeping the game scoreless. Following the barrage of shots, Ben O'Connor for the good guys finally regrouped and led his forwards up past center ice. The pass sailed to Stutzel; Alex and I trailed at both wing positions. I was at full speed by the home bench when *it* happened again, only in a different spot this time.

"Gah! No!" I gritted my teeth to erase the sight of Amy and bombed towards the net, unguarded. 'In front!' Michael rifled a pass forward which tipped off the head of my stick as I agonizingly collided with Minnesota's goaltender, sending us both tumbling into the sliding net (now off of its moorings). But through it all, the puck had beaten the defenseless goalie.

"Yeah! Yes yes yes!" Leaping up from the ice, I threw my hands up in celebration. "Ha haah!" My teammates surrounded me to butt my helmet while smiling.

A noise from the goal area could be heard from our joyous circle. TWEET TWEET! TWEEEEEET! The referee was chirping on his overused whistle with arms extended at both sides. "No goal!" TWEET!

Hide the children. It was at this moment that everything glued together in my head had snapped. I no longer had any semblance of control.

"What!? What are you talking about, 'no goal'?" I screamed, separating myself from the four others dressed in yellow jerseys. "It was in the net!"

"No goal," repeated head referee McCormick. "You were in the crease."

"In the—what kind of call is that!? Even you saw that I couldn't stop! That was a goal!"

"The goaltender was interfered with." McCormick glided over to the scorer's table to give his announcement. Yeah, I wasn't having that.

"Hey, what the hell ref? Don't walk away from me —you know that was a goal! What are you, a Minnesota hockey booster or something?" During the rant, my teammates attempted to calm me, as it was of no use. I quickly broke free of their restrain. "Fuck you McCormick!"

To spare you the rest of this humiliating argument, I was tossed from the game. The head zebra had had enough expletives for one night. The crowd 'booed' (mostly due to the disallowed goal) as I stormed off the ice, past my speechless team and down the tunnel to our locker room. I suddenly became dizzy, sweating from head to toe.

My helmet was violently thrown against an unfortunate locker in a fit of rage. Like I said, control had escaped and I knew not what I did; in fact, while driving back home that evening (electing not to remain on campus), I would ultimately realize what had occurred but still wouldn't believe it. How could an even-tempered guy like me go off the deep end? From severe anger, I would nearly fight off tears while sitting in our dressing room, dreading the period break where I would be joined by nineteen of my closest friends. I couldn't avoid it; my personal life had slipped into my athletic career.

*****

So, three engineers are sent down to hell. By request of the devil, they are to repair the plumbing, air conditioning, wiring, what have you. The devil has never been happier with the new appearance of his dungeon, however when god receives word of the activity happening below, he is outraged. "You send those men up here where they belong at once!" he orders to no avail. "I'll sue," claims god. "I'll get a lawyer!" The devil responds with, "Yeah, like your going to find any up there."

Sorry about that; I felt the need to cover up my misfortunes with some cheap humor. The truth was, a few days following the worst game of my young career, I *was* feeling a bit better. I made the decision to remain at Guiseppi's while driving out to hockey practice every other day (per order of Jerry Trodeau). Speaking of which, the coach had called me into his office the first Monday practice after my explosion. The meeting went similar to this:

"Take a seat son, I want to talk with you."

"Okay Coach," I replied, picking my words carefully. I surely knew what this would be about.

"How are things going for you Callie? Is school alright?"

"Huh? Oh yeah Coach, school is just fine."

"How about home? Are things all right there?"

"Yeah. Yeah, things are fine." I lied.

"Well, something is most definitely bothering you and I'd like to distinguish what it is. Maybe I can help you." He broke to take a sip of water from his blue UM mug. "Let me be frank, Dave. What I saw on Saturday was absolutely frightening and can get you in some serious trouble. I understand you have energy and a passion for the sport out there but you CANNOT exert it in that fashion. You're too talented a player to throw it away on silly arguments, fighting and what not. Are you sure nothing is going on?"

"Everything is good, I just lost my temper. It's just that—"

The coach put his hand up. "I know, I know. You're not the first player in my tenure to protest a bad call. And it *was* a bad call, I agree. But let it go. Channel that pent-up anger and use it later in the game to net a goal. Hell, you've got nine of them this year." Trodeau paused again while licking his lips, searching for the next sentence. Pushing his eyeglasses up his nose, Jerry stated; "Look Dave, you've fit in surprisingly well with the club this year. Don't ruin it."

"I'm sorry, sir, I promise it won't happen again."

"Good. And don't call me 'sir', 'coach' is fine. Come on now, get suited up for practice now."

I nodded my head and waltzed toward the door when Jerry spoke once again.

"One more thing, Callie. If you ever have a problem, relating to the team or not, please feel free to talk with me. My office is most always open."

"Thanks, I will."

It turned out that behind his commanding exterior, Jerry Trodeau was one of the good guy's in the world. I fully expected to walk into his coach's room to receive and all-out lynching and although he was noticeably upset with me, it turned out surprisingly pleasant.

So back to my previous statement, I stayed at Guiseppi's past my promised date as Steven had yet to find a new cook. I had actually offered to stay, opposed to Mr. Toscano begging me. I would soon find out that the less time spent alone—and my mind off of Amy—the better, who by the way, I still hadn't spoken to since Christmas (excluding that pathetic New Year's Eve conversation). When sitting by my lonesome, I would wonder what my girl was doing; where she currently was, if there was a boy she liked or was even seeing, if they were out somewhere, if they were kissing each other. You get the point. Senseless thoughts can enter one's mind when he or she isn't in the know. You think the worst and hope for the best.

Despite the fact that everyone loathes any type of *work*, I actually wasn't having a horrible time. Toscano continued to pay me good money under the table while treating me like a saint, as well he should. That particular Tuesday, I had mentioned to my boss that for the first time in over 2 years, I was single. He was very familiar with Amy from the past 30 months as frequently, she'd drop by our shop to visit or keep me company—so during this period, she and Steven became well acquainted.

"Oh Davie, my boy…you find somebody soon. Amy, she nice girl, but you find somebody better," was what the little Italian said to me. "You no worry."

"Thanks Mr. Toscano," I would reply. "But I'm not really looking."

My $350 personal checks proved to be handy at the close of every week, allowing me to pay my car insurance, credit card, and cellular phone bills, something I was prohibited from doing during the school year. It also enabled me to treat Mike and Alex to dinner following a team practice one evening. The three of us had really become brotherly like through the course of our season and it wasn't like a 'Mikey Brother' either. Maybe I should say we had become very close friends, which, I assumed, aided us on the ice as well. It was strange; the three of us being as different as we are, becoming buddies while shocking fans with our extreme level of play.

Alex was the youngster of the group, only eighteen, coming from a vast family of three sisters and two brothers (both of which were older and played collegiate hockey in years prior). He had a lot to live up to and due to this, Alex was an absolute workhorse in practice. The consequences arising from this was that the left-winger tended to be extremely hard on himself. Moreover, we often found him muttering obscenities to himself on the bench. Anyway, Alex constantly wanted to be at the top of his game with his brothers normally in attendance, watching him intensively. That must be demanding. If I failed to mention previously, Alex stood 5'11", about average size for a forward. He leaned towards the skeletal side, only making him faster and able to burn defensemen with ease.

My friend Stutz, on the other hand, was a towering center, standing six foot three, with more than enough fat to keep him toasty in the wintertime. He sported a nearly shaved head (while like myself, Alex had a full wig of bushy hair) and was ripped with muscles, reminiscent of Sean Collins. Mike was a very shy person, being an only child all of his twenty years. We were both first-year sophomores in terms of athletics at Michigan (really, our only similarity). Of the three amigos, Hutch traveled from the furthest distance, residing in Toledo, and obviously, stayed in the temporary housing set up for us. Still, we were all considered local boys.

Amidst our varied backgrounds, we acted as one on the ice. I'll have to admit, as ecstatic as I was to be placed with two rookies (not having to deal with the pressure of playing with upperclassmen), I never imagined we'd be enjoying the success that we were. Apparently, Trodeau had noticed something in us from start, making him that winning, well-respected coach.

Unfortunately, through the first part of January, our team had hit its first real losing streak of the season. After the victory by Minnesota on the sixth, we dropped back-to-back contests against Lake Superior State, really damaging us in the standings. On the nineteenth of

January, we finished in a 3-3 draw versus the Redhawks of Miami (Ohio), extending our current winless streak to four depressing games. My current point-less streak also sat at four. No goals, no assists; nothing. However, it wasn't solely me as the whole team struggled mightily, even the pompous Gerry Walsh. The Hoover and Marcus combined allowed some weak shots to trickle in and the defense certainly wasn't holding up their end of the bargain, letting opposing forwards dance right past them. See, this is why hockey teams on a roll despise an extended holiday break. All momentum we had gained prior to final examination week was lost.

The second Lake Superior loss dipped us to a lowly fourth in the Central Collegiate Hockey Association standings, trailing the conquering Lakers, Michigan State, and our archrival, the much-hated Buckeyes of Ohio State University. There were fewer than two months (approximately fourteen games, give or take a couple) remaining in our journey and if the Wolverines were to make a tournament push, this losing steak would have to end *now*. All too often college squads burst out of the gate like gangbusters only to fatigue long before the season is done. Knowing Trodeau & Associates, we were determined to prevent this from happening.

For some reason throughout my dismal slump, I couldn't shake the thought of Amy from my ever-churning mind. Well, I suppose I *did* know a portion of the reason. Obviously, I loved her once and still love her today, despite attempts to convince myself otherwise. She was my girlfriend for two and a half years. Two and a half damn years! There is an old saying that described the amount of time it takes to completely recover from a lost love, something like the number of months or years spent with that person divided by three—maybe it's not three, I don't know but in any case, it certainly wasn't now. I missed Amy Lewis incredibly and people near to me were beginning to take notice. The pain dug even deeper from not being able to talk with her, especially since I used to hear her beautiful voice every day of every week. It didn't matter if she was the busiest woman alive where every second was a struggle for free time to pick up that telephone. If she were on vacation; say, in Canada, Florida or even Budapest, my receiver would still ring its ring with a cheery girl on the other side. Boy oh boy, how those memories ripped me apart inside.

Somehow, someway, I would continue to do what I was doing; block the babe from my mind and focus on the important matters. She was just so helpful when it came to—NO! The only way to succeed was to leave the past behind and move on. Matters could only grow worse from dwelling. I was just so happy with her, knowing that—NO! Was it this difficult to *not* think about her for five seconds? Was it impossible? And speaking of impossible, Amy once won a track meet while infected with a killer cold. Ugh. I give up.

Sitting about the circular table at Zippy's that Monday evening, Stutz, Hutch and I lamented a bit over our lack of victories. There was really nothing else to discuss.

"I just can't understand it," mentioned Mike with his large hands pressed firmly against his forehead, "It's like everything that worked for us before all of a sudden doesn't."

An upbeat Alex chimed in. "I think it'll turn around soon. We didn't exactly play half-bad in that Michigan State game—just couldn't cash in on good opportunities. One of these games, it'll all click again."

"You think so, hmm?"

"I do. Perhaps even by the next game, it's going to come together."

"I hope so," I added from my edge of the table. "I'm sick of it."

A young waitress sauntered up to our table, a small pad of paper extended in one hand with a pen situated in her left ear. She smiled widely at the three college boys, trying to make a strong opening impression.

"Hullo guys, are you ready to order?"

"I believe so," spoke Mike. "I'll have a bacon burger, cooked medium-rare with fries."

"I'll get the Buffalo wings and umm…a side of nachos."

"And for you, sir?" The hostess made me feel important.

"I think I'll have the Southwest burger, medium-well."

"Very well, I'll put the order right in for you gentlemen."

Michael and Alex blatantly stared at the college waitress, strutting from our table to the kitchen. Her jet-black skirt rustled from side to side and exposed a good portion of her upper leg. She moved like a Victoria's Secret model, swaggering down the runway in a fashion show. Maybe that was in the job description.

"Man…oh man," remarked an excitable Alex, clearing the recently formed perspiration from his face.

"I bet she's nuts, if you know what I mean," spoke Mike rudely while winking.

"Oh come on guys!" said I. "She's not that special."

"You're honestly going to sit there and tell me she isn't attractive?"

I responded immediately with, "Yes!"

"You're crazy Callie. If you don't find that girl hot then nothing will ever strike you fancy. Oh wait a minute," thought Michael. "You're still caught up on 'what's her name'."

"Amy."

"Yeah, that's it. You have to get over her dude!" Here we go with the 'dudes' again; he must be taking grammar lessons from the captain.

"I am. Really, I am. I just fail to see what's so great about this girl."

Hutch and Stutz gave a collective sigh. "We need to find you a cute woman," spoke Alex. "Hey, what ever happened to that girl you slept with in Boston?"

"Whoa whoa whoa! Hold up! I never *slept* with her!"

The big center-man wasn't satisfied. "Sean told us you woke up in the same bed; naked, I presume?"

"No! Well, sort of. She was—I mean, I was—I mean, she—" I paused to collect my thoughts. "We were only *naked* from the waist up and I have no idea how we ended up that way." I spoke in an unobtrusive tone, careful that the neighboring tables wouldn't pick up the conversation.

"Yeah I bet, Casanova," joked Alex. "You had all the smooth moves going that night."

"Don't remind me."

"Maybe you should dial her up, she was pretty good-looking."

"Are you kidding? No way, I'll never see her face again."

"Just a suggestion."

It wasn't uncommon for a pack of high teens and younger twenty-something's to have these sexually oriented conversations. For one reason or another, most kids my age had nothing else on their minds but women, women and women. Thankfully, we also had hockey. So basically, if you put a woman on skates, it'd take days to calm us down.

The three of us yakked professional sports until the attractive waitress (at least in the eyes of the other two) delivered our food. Her beam was large as she slickly positioned the plates between our arms. This girl knew exactly how to get the tips.

"Can I get you gentlemen anything else?"

"We're all set, thank you," I answered as she began to slink away.

"Actually, excuse me one second," spoke Mike, seemingly up to something. What projected from his mouth then would embarrass me greatly (at least for the coming minutes). Had he no control over his speech? "Yes, excuse me...we were wondering if you think our friend here is good-looking?" asked he, waving a finger in my direction.

My faced turned thirteen shades of red as my eyes near flew out from the sockets. "Mike!" I spoke in the loudest whisper possible. "Shut up!"

"No seriously, he's been a little down on himself lately. Do you find him handsome?"

"I ahhh—" spoke the humiliated waitress. "I don't know what to say."

"Well, just tell us the truth. Attractive? Yes or no?" I threw my jacket over my head, covering it completely so as not to show myself in this most awkward episode.

"Normally I have to get to know somebody before I judge them," I heard the girl say.

But Mike simply wouldn't let go. "Well, just suppose he's a nice guy with a good personality, ok? Do you find him attractive?"

"I umm...like his hair and...well yes. Yes, I would say he's attractive. There, are you happy?" And she immediately vacated the area.

"Hah! Yes!" jumped Stutz. "Look at that! Who needs Amy, huh?" He began to sing: "Go Dave, it's your birthday—"

I finally revealed myself from the large winter coat. "Thanks a lot jackass. You just *had* to say something."

"But aren't you glad I did!? She digs you!"

"I bet she digs her boyfriend who bought her the huge ring on her finger too."

"What?"

"Exactly."

The embarrassing feelings soon passed and we were back to chumming again until 8:30 or thereabouts when we parted our separate ways; me driving back to Fenton. It was a dark, cloudy night as I drove down the near-deserted highway en route to my hometown. For the first time in weeks, a laugh overtook me just thinking about the dinner event. You know, it's great to have friends.

11

Sitting on our team's bench at the classic Yost, I observed our squad squaring off against an unfamiliar opponent. They wore a lime-colored uniform with a shade of orange painted on their helmets, making for a very unlikely combination. Their entire team appeared to be twice our size and skated faster, shot harder and body-checked our players with a force that drove them face-first onto the ice in a state of unbearable pain.

I watched as paramedics carted All-American, Gerry Walsh, off the rink with a stretcher and minutes later, Derek Strickland would suffer the same. The Wolverines were losing players left and right ("dropping like flies" was Trodeau's comment) as the crowd groaned with every new injury. I trembled on the bench while the coach swallowed a handful of Advil in one gulp. It seemed as if every time I blinked, something went terribly wrong. And sure enough at that moment, Sean Collins lumbered slowly off the ice, greatly favoring one leg. He opened his mouth and blood gushed out, followed by a few teeth plunging to my lap.

"We can't beat 'em...buddy," he managed to spit out before limping down the tunnel. I badly wished to follow him and even seriously considered it until:

"Calvetto! Get out there!" came Trodeau's booming voice into my ear. Has he lost his mind?

"I can't go in Coach, I'll get killed!"

"You get the hell in there or we'll have to forfeit the game!" The opposing players snarled at me from the ice and beckoned me to join the fun.

"Coach...no!" I muttered, my voice shaking. He then grabbed the back of my neck and attempted to hurl me into the game as I latched onto the boards for dear life.

The capacity crowd hooted wildly at this charade, all looking down and pointing. One male voice of laughter rose above all others. It was heard from beyond the ice, beyond the Plexiglas, in the first row of seats behind the visiting goal. He was an odd-looking man of about 21 whom I failed to recognize, however, the girl standing beside him was no foreign face. She too laughed like the rest while waving at me and shaking her head from left to right.

I held on to the nearside boards with all my might as I saw the loud-mouthed man turn towards Amy Lewis and passionately kiss her on the lips. He made certain to flash me his great big whites, saying through his mind, *tough shit pal, I've got her and you don't.*

"Amy! No! How can you do this to me!?"

"Calvetto! Let go! Get out there!"

"Amy!"

"Hahahahaha!"

"Amy, stop it! He's doesn't love you! Amy!"

I leapt from my soggy pillow, dripping with sweat all over. It still took a few minutes before I realized this was merely a horrible nightmare. A horrible nightmare! I sat straight upwards for the following minutes, replaying the images over and over in my mind as the alarm clock read 3:25 in the morning. Sleep was not a possibility for the remainder of the a.m.

This has totaled up to three nightmares now in three consecutive nights, and also for the third straight day, I would cut classes due to my brutal exhaustion. Not being able to sleep at the normal time made me drowsy during the afternoon hours, which my roommate Adley was beginning to notice. I guess it'd be impossible for him not to; me occupying the room the majority of the day. It was only the second week of classes and I had missed half of them already!

I should probably mention that I saw my ex-girlfriend strolling through a department store last weekend, most likely triggering my recent violent dreams. Talk about being uncomfortable. Thankfully, she walked alone as I probably would have gone mental seeing her with some chump. When I questioned if there was a special guy in her life, Amy refused to answer. Of course, as we all know, that could mean one of two things.

The two of us chatted for no more than ninety seconds. Amy looked as stunning as ever, maybe even more so now, with her hair cut shorter than I had remembered and styled in a chic fashion. She asked how I was holding up with the whole debacle, figuring I was worst-off between us, but I lied and claimed everything was just fine. Just fine! I wanted to make her miss me. I longed for her to come running back. I couldn't show weakness.

Since that Sunday afternoon at the store, my nightmares hadn't ceased. Amy's face was once again vivid and alive in my dreams; it's as if my brain took a snapshot of my former love, embedding it in there for me to revisit whenever my eyes closed. Seeing the girl only caused more pain.

The day at hand, January the 30th, would be one like no other. It began similar to any ordinary late morning, as giving up on sleep, I decided to attend my Psychology and Renaissance Literature lectures (dozing through the latter). I met up with Sean for lunch at the Northside Dining Hall about 12:30, returning to my dorm there after. It was a Tuesday.

Strolling back to my appropriate building, I envisioned my comfortable bed and of course, me laying in it. The showers went unused that morning. I decided to toss on a pair of sweats and to go class, a ritual I was beginning to follow almost daily. Little did I know that a visitor would be awaiting me back in the room.

Headphones covering my ears, I walked into our dormitory room singing some rap-ish song. I nearly leapt to the ceiling when encountering this unwelcome stranger. My roommate shrugged his shoulders.

"Tanya? What are you doing here!?"

"Well, good to see you too," the old memory sarcastically responded. She sat cross-legged on our blue futon, dressed in a dark sweater, blue jeans, long black boots and a jacket around her hourglass waist while her curly hair was tied back into a clip. Just as I remembered her from that weekend two months ago; a striking beauty. You know, only with clothes on.

"Wow!" was the only thing that came from my mouth.

Tanya lifted herself from the couch and gave me one of those fake girly hugs. Here I was, just days ago, figuring this girl was far too drunk to even remember who I was and where I lived. Now she was standing right here, arms around me. Wow was right.

"How did you find me?" I asked Tanya.

"Oh, I looked you up on the college website. Our team is up to play your school tonight and I figured since I'm here and all, I just had to come see you."

"I'm surprised you remembered me."

"How could I forget?"

"I don't know, you were a little—well—" and nothing else came out. I remained in disbelief.

"Uh!" Tanya gasped. "A little what, huh? Obviously, I'm not going to forget the night completely; that never happens." Oh boy. "And I don't sleep next to just anybody." Good gracious. Adley, now very much interested, wheeled around in his chair.

"I didn't mean it like that! Don't take me the wrong way here," I politely responded. "I just...well, I don't really know you too well. That's all."

Tanya stretched her cheekbones into a wide smile. It wasn't your ordinary smile either; to me, it shined like an underhanded, devilish, devious, bad-girl smirk. A smirk that brought forward all the bad hidden deep inside of her. A smile that made you want her.

"Hey, I can't stay long but we're playing a volleyball game tonight in your field house...um, I'm not sure which one."

"Probably Callamarri Arena, that's where the boy's V-ball teams plays."

"Yeah, that's it! Bring some of your hockey friends, it'll be great! You'll get to see all the girls again!" (None of whom I would even recognize).

Tanya delivered another squashing bear hug before she departed as I was more prepared for it this time. "Thanks for ah...visiting." I swung the heavy door shut following Ms. Aiken's stunning exit and shook my head, trying to return to my previous state.

"So who was that?" questioned my computer-nerdy roommate.

"Who knows?"

*****

Amy and Tanya. Tanya and Amy. Two opposite females. Two similar females. One lost, one found. One love, one lust. One dream, one nightmare. Both attractive. Both outspoken. Both the same. Both different.

Perhaps it's the undeniable fact that I missed Amy beyond words and wasn't ready for someone new, because Tanya was there for the plucking and I wasn't interested. She stood even more picturesque than I remembered with the darker skin and absolutely perfect body. What was wrong with me? I know it's highly uncommon for a guy to be stuck up on one single lady, but as you've most likely realized by now, I'm no ordinary dude.

So based on this, I probably failed to attend Tanya's game, didn't I? Well, you're wrong. I managed to gather a troupe of teammates (not being able to handle myself alone) who reluctantly tagged along. Playing the roles of bastards, we routed against our school and cheered on the girls in orange for the evening. Having never been to a true volleyball game, we also demonstrated the role of village idiots. "Yeah! Hit the ball! Get it over the net! Win the game! Go! Go! Go!"

Hey, we were hockey players, what do you want?

Our old one-nighter friends from 'Cuse rolled to victory (by some score I couldn't understand) as I guessed UM's volleyball team didn't parallel its other strong athletic sports. I can't honestly say that women's V-ball is the talk of the campus. If anything, the team makes the back page of the in depth sports section with no pictures being taken of them. Anyway, Tanya's winning squad would return to New York after a few minutes spent reminiscing with us. Our crew chatted with theirs while Amy's opposition hung from me like a monkey on bars. I enjoyed it, but at the same time didn't. It's almost as if my friends envied me and I only wish I envied myself. At least my near-tarnished image had recuperated.

During those few uplifting self-conscious minutes, my rotten luck would only grow far shoddier though. Oh, how I wished Tanya remained a ghost from the past; left and forgotten about in the city of Boston. Just not here. Not now. For in those short minutes preceding Syracuse's departure, those untimely, inopportune minutes, my cellular phone rang. I knew full well that by not answering, it might never happen again.

Guarding myself from the rest, I softly spoke to Amy, keeping my voice low and out of range from Ms. Aiken. Amy seemed unsure of herself; unsure of why she called and unsure of my tone. I wished to be in the luxuries of my home, where I could speak freely and express myself without distractions. So what was the problem, you ask? Our conversation was breezing along fine (or as well as could be expected) until Tanya opened her big mouth. "Who are you talking to Davie? Your girrrrrlfriend?" Remember, she didn't even know Amy existed or the in-depth story that corresponded. I attempted to walk away, batting my hand in hopes she'd get the hint. "Is that your girlfriend Dave? Huh? Huh? Is it? You ladies' man, you!"

Just as I expected, Amy asked: "Who's that?" before I had created a suitable answer. "Oh, I see how things are. It looks like I'm non-existent these days. Sorry I called!" Click. Dial tone.

That night, while lying awake for the fourth straight sleepless night, I would eventually realize something important—a revelation that took only the most uneducated man on the face of the earth not to figure out. Tanya is an idiot.

*****

On the final day of January, I spent the small number of minutes between classes on my favorite wooden bench, soon becoming a practice for me. No drawings were sketched this day, as I wasn't exactly in the correct mood. You see, the previous evening was spent sending message after message to my infuriated ex-girlfriend, trying to convince her that there was no woman in my life. And the worst part was, this was no lie. I formulated some crazy story involving Sean and a retarded lady-friend of his that felt the dire need to annoy me while on the phone. "She must have tourettes or something," I tried saying on the answering machine. I doubted she would buy it. But why was I attempting to cover myself up? Wasn't Amy the one who unchained herself from me? Why should she be mad and accuse me of finding a replacement? It made no sense.

That particular mild-weather afternoon, I didn't take notice of the normal campus sights. No, instead my mind reeled and tossed and turned and tottered, completely engulfing it from the present world. So I failed to take notice of the pond, the swaying trees, the passing cars in the distance, the traditional (even in winter) Frisbee game, even the students waving to me as they strolled by. I was oblivious. However, it was at this present time on this present day that I derived my genius plan. This plan was perfect and was a sure bet to get my former love back. Oh yes! In fact, I would dedicate my entire Renaissance Literature class (the new one at the 1:30 time slot for the semester) to preparing a scheme and jotting down photographic details for this strategy of mine. It served as a pleasant disruption from the doths and how art thou's of class.

The hockey squad would take to the Yost's ice for an unusual Wednesday evening match up that night in hopes of ending our miserable winless streak. We were to arrive at the rink no later than 4 p.m. for additional warm-up time. Trodeau and the staff had grown tired of the sub-par play, so naturally, more was demanded of us. I had only 1 hour between classes and practice to nap, shower, dress myself, pack up my hockey gear and walk the 10-minute trek down the hill to the arena. My alarm clock would screech only twelve minutes after sleep grabbed me and come game time, I was fairly lightheaded from the drowsiness. Somebody ask Trodeau how a simple weekday hockey game can turn into a near six-hour event. That's grueling for even the best of the best. But I had come much too far, worked much too hard and had established a sense of responsibility and reliance to simply hang up the skates. The thought would never cross my mind. I had a place with this team and without every piece, the puzzle would not be complete.

This would finally be the night where my pointless streak would come to a long-awaited finish.

February 2003

12

A load was lifted from our shoulders by not only winning on January 31st but emerging victorious on the 3rd of February as well. The locker room morale had risen and in my mind, the team had returned to its championship pedestal, climbing up the standings. We passed Lake Superior State once again, moving to third position with 33 points, still trailing the Spartans and red-hot Ohio State who sat at 42, setting the stage for a primo February 16th and 17th weekend match-up at Columbus. It would easily be the largest, most anticipated weekend of the season. Let's just hope I don't meet some easy Buckeye girl.

On Thursday afternoon (the 8th), I received a package in the lobby of my dormitory, addressed from 74 Hancock Street in Fenton. Upon arrival back in my room, I tore the duct tape from the brown box and pulled out two Tupperware containers, accompanied by a letter. 'Davie' was written in big blue letters on the envelope.

Hello Davie,

I thought you might want some snacks for the room so I baked you oatmeal cookies and some brownies. Be sure to share.

I hope all your classes are going well and you've been able to find time for homework. I just wanted to let you know, your father and I are very proud of you for handling this Amy situation well. It's very hard, she was a nice girl.

Let us know when you're coming home...we'll be out at the end of the month for the February 23rd game. Good luck this weekend. Don't get hurt.

Love,
—MOM

"Don't get hurt." This was Mom's usual plea before every game, even dating back to high school. With every life-threatening hockey accident across the world, it was a mother's fear the same would happen to their child.

I took the two containers, filled with homemade brownies and cookies, and placed them in the wooden armoire on the far corner of the room. College students live for care packages. We cherish all snacks prepared by our parents, basically because the dining hall's food is so atrocious. Many nights, we're unsure what it is exactly that's being scooped onto our trays.

The boys and I would walk down to the Crisler Arena that thirsty Thursday for an exciting men's basketball game. Figuring b-ball was far more popular than ice hockey, the construction crew built 14,000 extra seats in their arena than they did next door at the Yost. The Michigan basketball squad had a lot more history ('The Fab Five', 'The House That Cazzie Built', 1989's overtime championship victory etc.) and dated back much further than us (the Yost Arena was originally built for basketball) so I dealt with the larger place without argument. The Crisler was bigger than half the NBA arenas around the country, however, which was a big extreme for a Big Ten school.

The house only sold 9,000 tickets by the eight o'clock tip-off, barely filling the large lower deck; the balcony was nearly deserted. I had my roommate and his friends save us five seats in the student section above the home team's bench as knowing Alex, and especially Derek, we'd be late. And just as I expected, we were.

It was twenty past when we graced everybody with our presence. Entering from the top of the section, I spotted Adley with five unoccupied stadium seats beside him and led the charge down the concrete stairs. The crowd situated in the nearby area began to clap their hands and hoot, not uncommon for a sporting event, but one thing was odd. The basketball game was currently on a timeout. As I glanced around at the cheering fans, they weren't even focused on the court, not even at the giant scoreboard. Instead, all heads and clapping hands were directed towards the five of us (Alex, Sean, Marc, Derek and myself), making us stop short, stunned at the ovation.

"Thank you. Thank you so much, we love you all," preached Alex while taking a bow. "Really now, you're all too kind!"

The rest of us waved a hand in the air as a token of gratitude. Derek smoothly tipped his gray hat at the people, knowing full well that being a minority ice hockey athlete made him a fan favorite. He was also a lady's favorite, something I envied.

Feeling mighty embarrassed, I slinked into the empty row of seats next to Adley.

"You always know how to make an entrance, don't you?" remarked my roommate, less than amused.

"Thanks for saving our spot."

"Don't mention it."

The buzzer sounded in the enormous arena and the teams began play once again. Oh, why couldn't Amy have been with me during our entrance? She'd be so impressed! Seeing how kids and grown-ups alike treated me like a superstar would have her latched to my side. Amy would address publicly that she were "the loving girlfriend of this prodigious hero" to boost her character. If only she were here. If only she could understand.

The boys and I routed on our disappointing home team after the timeout but soon after, an older man, dressed in a heavy jacket and driver's cap with a younger child at his side, interrupted us all.

"Excuse me fellers. If it's not too much trouble, my grandson would like your autographs."

"No problem!" beamed Alex from the end of the row, who was simply living the dream. He signed the boy's basketball program and passed it down the line for the rest to follow. I couldn't believe my signature was valuable at this moment; five months ago, anyone outside of Fenton wouldn't recognize my name on a piece of paper. It's funny how things can change with the snap of two fingers.

I signed the boy's program in the slowest of fashions, wanting to write every letter in perfect style. Let's face it; I hadn't taken 'Autograph Signing 101' in school yet. So, after sending the program back down the row, I continued to watch the b-ball game until another disruption occurred. It was a tapping on my shoulder.

"You're David Calvetto from the hockey team, right?" came the voice of another younger child, this one I guessed to be between the ages of ten and twelve. He sat in the row behind us with two vacant seats on either side (probably from escaping parents). "Yeah, yeah, I know you! My daddy and I watch all the games! Wow ! I can't…I can't believe you're right here!"

"Well, I am human, kid," I spoke to the adolescent, turning back around to face Chrisler's court. Sean and I exchanged humorous looks.

"Yeah, so I saw that game when you scored two goals," continued my new friend. "Totally awesome! The first one was cool and all but that second goal—oh man! You really faked out that defenseman. You got him good!"

Without facing the young fan, I said; "Yep, I sure did."

"So…so do you think you'll win the champemchip—I mean championship this year?" Why wouldn't he shut up? "I mean you guys have lost a few games and everything."

"We'll be fine."

"What's that?" spoke this kid, his voice growing louder with every second. This was really starting to irritate me.

"I said 'we'll be fine'."

"Oh." The child finally closed his mouth. Perhaps he took the hint that I didn't want to hear his ridiculous questions or comments anymore. 'I am human, kid,' here like the other nine thousand to enjoy a basketball game. "So my daddy says that—"

"Come on kid, leave him alone for Christ's sake," butted in my chum beside me.

"Wow!" exclaimed the Mickey Mouse Club's number one member at top volume. "You're Sean Collins!"

*****

Thursday's page was ripped off the calendar, now reading Friday, February 9th. Execution day. My plan would finally be carried out close to 11 p.m. as surprisingly, over the nine days since I derived it, I never second-guessed or even considered backing out. It was completely foolish to anybody with even a trace of morals or dignity. As I've mentioned before, it seemed perfectly right to me. Sadly. I was a lost man without my Amy. I didn't want Tanya, not the waitress at Zippy's, not Elizabeth; nobody but Amy Lewis who, for all I knew, could be devoting her love to some lucky Bowling Green man. And if there was a guy, he should be damn thankful for attending an Ohio university or I'd track him down and kill him. Well, not kill him in the literal sense but maybe knock him around a bit; show him who's boss. I wouldn't feel guilty either; nope, I wouldn't. This was the man I had become.

Back to reality, I worked a difficult 4-close shift at Guiseppi's following my final Friday classes. I knew from experience that Friday's bring in the most cash of any day with upwards of three to four thousand sitting in the register at closing time. Owner Toscano cleared his drawer prior to departing every day, leaving only fifty dollars in fives, ones and coins for the following morning. He managed a business very successfully.

Customers came and went that evening as I diligently prepared their food and money was deposited into the register. I grew excited with every ringing *cha-ching*. The two cashiers (and order-takers) worked extra hard that night; seventeen-year-old Meghan and the older Sandy currently on staff. Occasionally, a grunt or grown could be heard from their direction as one would stop, breath deep, run a hand through their hair, then finally continue the job. Steve and I worked the entire night without a single break.

From the years of being employed, I knew this place in and out. I knew that Mr. Toscano locked the front doors at precisely 10:59 (without fail) and it took four to five minutes to get all the customers out; I'd say 11:03 or 11:04, the shop would be empty. Meghan, being underage, was forced to leave at ten, therefore Sandy most always closed up with her boss - the same routine every night. Once the shop's analog clock read 11:05, Steven and Sandy, like every night preceding this once, would slip out back for a quick, relaxing cigarette. They would spend exactly two and a half minutes before returning to the back room to clean up, count and balance the register, and various other closing activities. The lights would be flicked off at 11:25.

After I shut down the grill, wild mischievous look upon my face, I strolled from the work area, past the rear door and into the narrow hallway where I deposited my dirty Guiseppi's smock into the sliding closet. My watch printed 11:03. Through the darkness of the corridor, I heard the creaking of a swinging door and a babbling Sandy, her voice trailing away.

"I'm going to enjoy this smoke tonight…" she excitedly remarked. And then SLAM; the door was shut. They were early.

My backpack and jacket lay on the floor of the gloomy closet, which I quickly grabbed and stumbled down the unlit hallway, one item under each arm. 'What a night,' complained Sandy from behind the thick door as I thought to myself, *Just wait, you've seen nothing.* I surveyed the kitchen to assume its emptiness, feeling like a grade-A thief. Soon enough, I would be.

Underneath my long shirtsleeve (on the bare wrist) sat a green stretch cord with three keys attached to it; one to unlock the front double doors, one for the stingy bathroom, and one to open to stores' cash register. Mr. Toscano had returned the set to me back in December, extending his complete trust. We were Italian Brothers. However, at this very moment, Steven's brother could be found tiptoeing past the idle grill to reach his intended target, inserting the appropriate key into the slot.

"Cha-Ching!" sounded the noisy register as I stopped short to make certain it was unheard by the authority outdoors. I waited ten seconds before inaudibly unzipping my school bag. My allotted time had reached one minute. The cash, just as I had suspected, packed every slot in its holder, with a mountain of twenties towering above the rest. My eyes bulged and my tongue protruded looking at the stacks of non-sequential bills, just sitting peacefully; waiting, wishing to be spent. Lousy pieces of printed paper! Lousy, incredibly meaningful, pieces of printed paper! Unguarded.

Gritting my teeth, I dug my hand in and grabbed a fistful of twenty-dollar bills, throwing them quickly into my opened sack. I repeated this process a second time and on the third, took all ten's from the opened drawer. The lower-valued bills (fives and ones) would be left behind for Steven and Sandy to stare at in amazement. Quickly, I pushed the register drawer back in (making another 'dinging' sound), removed my key from the hole, and zipped up the knapsack, swinging it around my shoulder. All evidence had been cleared. Despite my acquaintance with Sandy, she would most definitely have to receive the blame for this act. Hey, as far as I know, *Sandy must have made a huge mathematical or keying error, considering she was the only one operating the machine.* Sorry babe, that's life.

The back door swayed open nearly one full minute after my strike as Steve and his employee waltzed back in, completely unaware of what had happened beyond the door. I already had my coat on and was misleadingly rummaging around back at the starting point; the sliding closet. This was so easy, almost too easy. I wasn't even as satisfied as previously expected.

"Hey Steven, do you mind if I take off early tonight? I have a bunch of work to get done before Monday."

"Yes, yes Davie, it's okay," responded the now relaxed owner to me.

"The grill is shut down and the area is clean."

"Ah, thank you so much. You have nice night!"

"So long Dave, goodnight," wished a friendly Sandy.

With that, I smoothly ambled out of the lonesome restaurant, backpack hanging over my shoulder containing over eight hundred dollars of the day's revenue.

*****

So why did I do it, you ask. That's a fair enough question but I can't tell you the answer just yet. I'll only explain that Guiseppi's paychecks cover bills; tuition, car insurance, cell phone, schoolbooks, you name it, I pay it. These eight hundred and ninety dollars would be geared towards other uses.

I called in sick from work the following two days as Saturday was for a legitimate reason (family wedding in Dundee; some cousin of a cousin of a cousin) and Sunday would be most frightening at the shop, with Steven ripping his already thinning hair out, searching high and low for the missing money. I wanted no part of the accusations slapped down on the entire staff. Don't think I was stupid either; directly after shutting and locking the register drawer, I placed my key chain, containing all three keys, in Sandy's cabinet located in the break room. I tucked them in the back, behind all of her junk and out of sight from any rapid-moving eye. I made this maneuver prior to Steven and Sandy's reentry with plenty of time to spare. If accused of the crime, I would claim my cash register key had been lost or stolen some weeks ago.

What I also failed to mention occurred half a minute preceding my robbery in the dark coat closet. While grabbing my parka and knapsack, I slipped a pair of leather gloves (purchased from my trip to the department store where Amy unfortunately shopped as well) onto both hands. These remained on until I was safely behind the wheel of my Honda, driving down Riendeau Boulevard in the dark of night. No fingerprints would be traced to the scene of the crime. Like I mentioned, as far as I'm concerned, Sandy made an enormous error (or possibly a burglary). It's highly unlike me to commit this wicked, immoral act but hopefully you'll soon understand.

Dinner was prepared and served minutes after three o'clock at the Calvetto household: tortellini macaroni, meatballs and garlic bread were all on the menu, as I would follow my normal weekend routine by leaving for school shortly after we ate, getting me on campus before dark. It was strange being away from Ann Arbor for two full days. College athletes grow accustomed to games every weekend and a break in the schedule leaves them wondering how to spend their time. Most take it easy and catch up on rest. I steal money. Thinking about the robbery made me wonder if any of my hockey comrades ever pulled shit close to this. I doubted my close friends would; Sean, Alex and Mike didn't seem the type. What about Gerry? He was surely crooked enough to break the law but his All-American image would forever overshadow that. I imagined foreign-born Janni Perner and Marcus Pellenisius would never dream of stealing from good, innocent people. Derek, Eric Lessard and Marc DeSchriver seemed much too nice. Hooden was a team leader with focused goals and a very likable personality, eliminating him. Jeff Thomas (our 2nd line center man) had a bit of a rough image, bearing a tattoo on both his biceps, however I wouldn't pass judgment on him since we weren't too familiar with each other. How about the coaching staff? Perhaps our own dictator once stole as a kid or maybe Mr. Ridley ran into trouble with the cops in a past life. It was possible. I'm sure when applying for coaching positions, record of a thieved toy from Kaybee at the age of ten wasn't brought forth to the table and it surely didn't deny them the job. And I'm positive, if by stroke of genius I was somehow caught wouldn't bond me for life either.

Now that I've completely lost my train of thought, where the heck was I? Oh yes, the Sunday family dinner. Well, nothing exciting occurred at the table other than chitchat regarding Dad's business, Mom's concerns over everything under the sun, Mikey's pointless crap and few points regarding my education. In short, absolutely nothing interesting. Mom insisted that we have some "quality family time" before I headed back and Mikey locked himself upstairs in his room for the evening. We all played a rousing game of UNO; an extremely simple card game full of colors for suits, skips, reverses, draw twos, draw fours and wilds. "Fun For The Whole Family," explained the box in a marketing tactic, "Up To Ten Players!" How wildly exciting!

After winning the first hand, I shuffled and dealt the cards, seven to each player, around the freshly cleaned dinner table. One to Mom, one to Dad, one flicked at Mikey's face. One to Mom, one to Dad, one side-armed at Mikey's neck.

"Quit it!" he yelled.

"David, stop that." I received humor from this. Eighteen years of tormenting my younger brother and it never grew old.

The UNO cards were handed out and Mom began by throwing down the red six. Dad followed by lazily playing a red four, the perfect setup for Mike as he slapped a skip into the cardholder, sending the next move over to Mom. Oh well. Both parents again played red cards with Mikey, this time, slinging a reverse into the black holder. I gave out a deep sigh. This game was dumb.

I failed to pay attention as the rotation switched again and Mikey pitched a wild draw four onto the table.

"You jerk."

"Pick 'em up!" I had eleven cards in my hand now, none of any value; eight numbered cards, two skips and a draw two. The suit was switched to blue (I owned five of these) by my brother; the person who plays the wild card gets to choose the new suit, one of the silly rules. The game continued with my mother and father playing blues and Mikey, while looking at me and snickering to himself, unveiled another damn draw four.

"What *is* this?" I asked, getting impatient over the ridiculous game. "Are you cheating? I bet you are, show me your cards."

My mother laughed (Dad couldn't care less) as I failed to see what was so funny. I attempted to fan fifteen cards out before my face, knowing I'd probably never play one. Why couldn't I just drive back to school rather than suffer through 'quality family time'?

"Hah! Draw two!" yelled my immature brother.

"What?" Apparently, I again lost concentration as Mikey hit another skunk card on me. I had had enough. "You're cheating asshole!" I exclaimed, whacking his cards with my left hand, making them spill onto the table and floor. I released my fifteen in rage as they too cluttered the area.

"David!"

"What is your problem!?" snorted Mikey; both eyebrows sloped down to the peak of his nose. "You just can't take losing, can you? Give me a break, I hope you throw your stick when you lose the game for the hockey team too." That was it. I leaped to my feet with such a tremendous force that the wooden chair fell hard backwards, crashing against the floor. Before Mike could get up in defense of himself, I took my right arm and thrust it into the pit of his chest in a shoving motion. He, along with his chair, hit the tile floor with an incredible thumping sound. THUD! My brother, as if shot from a cannon, exploded to his feet, wanting to punch me good (maybe even draw blood) and raised his clenched fist to complete the task. I threw my elbows up in protection, bracing for the strike but it never came. Instead, when uncovering my eyes, my peacemaking father had Mike's fist closed in his enormous hand, standing between the two of us.

"Go to your room, now!" he ordered.

"Why should I? Dave started it!"

"Now!"

The little hellion swore as he surrendered and left the dining room in a tantrum. Before Mikey reached the base of the staircase, he delivered the last words. "Why don't you just stay at school? Explain why you need to come home and torture us!?"

"That's enough! Get up there!"

I quickly removed myself from the dining room to gather my last-minute belongings for the trip to Ann Arbor. I had to get out of there before the wrath was unleashed upon me.

"Hold on there tough guy," spoke my father. "What the hell was that all about?" I didn't answer but rather continued to immerse myself in packing. "Speak up, what's been your problem lately?"

"Nothing," I muttered, unable to look him in the eye. My suitcase full of freshly washed clothes sat by the front door and the plastic bag full of toiletries were now ready to go.

"It doesn't seem like nothing. You have this horrendous attitude about everything lately and we're starting to grow sick of it! Before you know it, this new temper will get your butt kicked off the hockey team so fast, you won't even realize it happened. What a waste of talent that'd be. Unbelievable. So you better find a damn good way to control yourself, mister." During Dad's rant, my mother had vacated the room to go calm Mikey. They have both performed this since the two brothers were young kids; one dealing with one troublemaker, settling him and laying down the punishment while the other parent took the second child. "Does this whole new-found temper thing pertain to Amy? Because if it does—"

"No, it doesn't! But hey, thanks for bringing her name up! Much appreciated!" What a jerk. "Look, I'm out of here. Tell Mom I said goodbye."

"David, hold on—"

I snatched my suitcase with the bag full of supplies in the same hand and flung open the door, storming out through the porch to the driveway, never looking back. This was the longest drive to school I had ever faced.

13

LOCAL RESTAURANT ROBBED OF MONEY: SECURITY CAMERAS TO BE INSTALLED

A family favorite, Guiseppi's Pizzeria & Calzones, was presumably robbed on the evening of Friday, February 9th, with over $850 stolen from the store's cash register. Police were brought to the scene and all cashiers were taken in for questioning, all clearly passing the lie detector test. "The drawer must have been ajar with its back turned upon," quoted shop owner, Steven Toscano, "I can't believe some untrustworthy customer would take that much money. It's an outrage."

Toscano, 47. has owned and maintained his local shop for twenty-one years. A husband of twenty-six years, Steven resides in Fenton with his wife, Gertrude, and his two children, Phillip and Isabella, sixteen and twelve respectively.

This is the 2nd reported robbery in two weeks with A&D Convenience held up on January 31st.

—Clint Berube is a Lake Area Times Columnist

WOLVERINES SET FOR OHIO STATE

The second place Michigan Wolverines travel to Columbus this weekend for two critical division match-ups against hated rival, Ohio State. The Buckeyes enter Saturday's contest with a 20-4-5 record; ranked third nationally (1st place CCHA). Michigan (17-8-4) trails OSU by seven points in their division and can reduce the gap to only three at weekend's close.

It has been an up and down season for Trodeau's 2002-2003 crew, from a season opening seven game win streak to a most recent five game winless stretch, dropping them in the standings. Back-to-back victories (3-2 over Miami, 6-2 over Nebraska-Omaha) have propelled the squad into third place, jumping past the Lakers of Lake Superior State. However, in the Mavericks game, fourth line freshman winger, Joseph Vitek, exited early with a mild concussion, sidelining him for approximately 2-3 weeks. In his place, Kevin LaFountain, 19, has been called up from the practice squad.

The Michigan-Ohio State rivalry has dated back to 1887, making it one of the oldest in collegiate athletics and certainly unlike any other. OSU hockey coach, Maurice Avulette, describes the rivalry as "the battle of north versus south where the coaches are the commanding generals and the players, ammunition. Endless round are fired upon order until only one side remains standing...and we crown them the victor."

This will be the 142nd meeting between the two schools with the Wolverines leading the overall series 71-59-12.

—Nancy Kelleher is a Lake Area Times Columnist

14

I tucked Friday's Times underneath the seat in front of me after reading (or skimming) nearly the entire thing, cover to cover. It occupied only one hour of the 250-minute bus ride from campus to Columbus, Ohio. Sadly, I had forgotten my headphones. Hey, who honestly has their head screwed on straight at seven o'clock in the bloody morning—especially when you participate in an "Anti-Ohio State" candlelight ritual the previous evening and far into the AM. Again, it's a rivalry "unlike any other," according to Nancy Kelleher.

Berube's article had made the final page of the local news section, hidden away in the bottom right corner, directly below a larger Holiday Inn ad. Readers would most likely scan by the editorial were they not looking directly for it. Apparently, about 32 pieces of news superseded the minor robbery (which wasn't even confirmed a robbery) in that thick portion of the paper. Flipping ahead three sections, the headline that read "Wolverines Set For Ohio State" sat in big, bold letters upon the front page of SPORTS. This was an example of news-making at its finest. The daily newspaper subscriber would much rather be educated on the weekend's college hockey match up than the local crime wave sweeping their beloved town. Does that make sense to you? Good, it doesn't to me either.

I awoke as our bus wheeled into the large OSU parking lot at a quarter to one that sunny Friday afternoon. Normally, my eyes failed to pop right open but this was a huge exception. Sean and I, sitting side-by-side and catching sight of the scene at the exact time, took a serious double take as we guessed word had seeped out as to the time and whereabouts of our arrival. We stared out the window in disbelief at the one hundred or so students grouped in a cluster, some holding picket signs reading; "Go Home UM," "Welcome To Hell" and of course, "Go Buckeyes." They began to grow more active as our vehicle pulled into an unloading space.

"Jesus!" remarked Sean.

"Exactly what I was thinking."

The bitter Michigan-Ohio State rivalry was far fiercer than I anticipated. Football, I could understand, and even basketball, but hockey? It's a sport that only dominates in the Northeast, Lakes Area, Colorado and portions of Alaska at the collegiate level. Why did these one hundred students skipping class give a damn? Perhaps the crazed mob simply despised everything from or relating to the state of Michigan.

"All right boys, we're here," announced Mr. Blemenson. Other eyes unlocked through the interior of the bus as my teammates groggily rolled their heads in an effort to rouse. The candlelight ritual (mixed with heavy drinking) took its toll on us all. "Hang tight here for one minute, we're going to see what the commotion is all about."

I got my first glimpse of the Value City Arena where 17,500 rowdy fans would gather hours later for the intense game. The building was absolutely immense; closer to a scale of the humongous Crisler rather than our dwarfed Yost. *There's no way this barn will fill*, I thought, gazing at the campus' landmark structure. However, come seven o'clock, all seats were occupied, including 400 sold to Michigan students, fans and Dekers who would sit behind the north goal. Little did I know, Amy Lewis would be among those in our respective section; and this wouldn't be a dream.

"Okay boys, lets unload. Take the stairs up to the rink and wait for us by the main double doors.... Don't leave anything behind." Announcer Blemenson paused to peer out the bus's opened door and retracted his statement by saying, "On second thought, wait up, here comes a police escort."

The bunch of us jerked our heads out the passenger's side windows to stare in awe at the oncoming horses, mounted with uniformed campus police. They hollered something to the unruly students and plowed their way through the parting group to our bus. I counted two, no three of them half-galloping this way.

"Clear the area! Clear this area right now!" I heard one cop yell through the bus' opened door. The crowd quieted but did not disband.

"Go home Michigan!"

"Get out of Ohio!"

"Clear this area!"

One policeman halted his horse at our door and pronounced to Coach Trodeau; "Send your team out, we'll walk one guy in front and one in back. You'll be safe." How reassuring.

The first-years all looked at each other wide-eyed, having seen nothing of this magnitude in their hockey careers while the team veterans wore a same-old-shit expression. I wondered if my Michigan campus would react the same when an OSU athletic team pays a visit. More than likely, yes. I remember watching the Michigan-Ohio State games with my father and brother as a child and listening to the old, classic announcers comment on the "ardent, acrimonious rivalry that pits an entire state up against the other." I guess the newspaper didn't lie. I was now living the rivalry, participating in the rivalry, even adding to the rivalry for future generations to read about!

"Okay boys," spoke Trodeau now, interrupting my running thoughts. "Let's head out. Ignore what's going on around you; we have a game to play tonight."

*****

Amy passed through the turnstiles of the Value City Arena, with friend Christophe by her side, fifteen minutes prior to face-off. The drive from Bowling Green to reach the capital took two hours by way of the '96 Ford Escort, which when driven by Amy, moved right along. Don't ask me what possessed these two lunatics to spare a fun-filled Friday evening or why they journeyed all this way (especially Christophe) to see an ex-boyfriend who just happens to skate for the opposition. She wouldn't have wasted the time when we were together. I wondered how she managed to score two tickets as well (from the ice-level, it appeared the house was full to the rafters with fanatical Buckeyes). Fanatical, arrogant, unintelligent, vociferous, rioting, repulsive, good-for-nothing Buckeyes. Resembling our sea of blue mixed with yellow at the Yost, the 17,000-plus stubborn sons of bitches all wore red at OSU games to distract the visiting team (often, it succeeded). Shortly following the game, I would also ask myself: *If Amy hated me so much, why did she and 'what's-his-name' wait for me at the player's exit?* Well, actually that quote arose shortly after the shock wore off. It happened like this:

The victors and I showered up and packed our equipment before leaving as a group for Columbus West High School (to save the school money, we were deprived of a nice, cozy hotel room in exchange for one luxurious night on a gymnasium floor). Water dripped from my uncut hair while I emerged from the shower stalls, falling into my clean, gray shirt (which I had just pulled down over my head), dampening the chest area in a dark, oval shape. The tee clung between both pectorals and protruded my large muscles. Yeah baby. I carefully walked barefoot down the wet locker room floor while soaking up the night's victory in my mind. *That'll teach those Buckeyes you can't compete with the big blue.* I threw on a pair of blue jeans, hung scrappily in my locker, along with boots and my black 'Michigan Hockey' windbreaker with two sticks in its logo before joining the jazzed crew at the steamy room's doors.

It took us until overtime but we departed the VC Arena a 4-3 winner on the wings of a Janni Perner rebound goal merely fifty seconds into the extra frame. Our bench erupted when the biscuit hit the basket while disappointed students launched programs and such onto our end of the ice. The busy police may have even cuffed one or two. In any case, the squad (along with our joyous 400 followers) enjoyed the hard-earned victory and shut up the first-place enemy, at least for the next twenty-one hours. In the words of Trodeau, "Don't get ahead of yourselves boys. This team still has a leg up in the standings so let's settle down, get a night's rest and be ready to roll again in the morning; nine o'clock on the high school rink. Be prepared to work. Good win tonight, let's keep it up."

The twenty seven of us (coaching staff, equipment manager, and injured Joseph Vitek included) left the friendly arena in a pack out the rear double doors and into the cool February evening air. The spectators had long fled the nearby parking areas, leaving only darkness occupying the street and sidewalks before us. Through my teammates' shoulders, I could spot two shady figures standing thirty feet ahead, across the deserted street. They stood alone.

Chumming with Alex, duffle bag strapped over my shoulder, stick heads pointing out at one unzipped end, we ambled across the empty access road and strode towards the dark parking lot where our diesel-filled carriage awaited. From underneath a streetlight came the shadowy gangster figures, approaching our group from the left.

"Here he comes. That's him right there," spoke Bonnie, pointing me out to Clyde. "David! Over here!" It was at that moment when I froze solid, seeing Amy in the wide beam of light. Ben O'Connor nearly rammed straight into my back, not anticipating my sudden halt in motion.

As I stood there stone-faced, thinking, *Why were Amy and 'what's his name' waiting for me at the player's exit?*, my ex came up to me, extending her thin arms around my waist and squeezing. The grasp wasn't as firm as it once was in the days of Amy and I, Calvetto and Lewis, boyfriend and girlfriend. "Great game tonight, David," She remarked, quickly terminating the hug. "Congratulations on the goal!"

All I could speak was, "Amy? Wha-what are you…Amy?"

"Yes it's me, don't be so shocked. This is my friend Christophe from school," remarked the beauty, dressed in her normal black, puffy bubble coat with a white headband covering her ears and resting on the hairline. Her cheeks were a rosy red shade from the brisk wind whipping out of the west and a light tear clouded up her right eye. For the first time in what seemed an eternity, I gazed at Amy's curled lips; her two dimples, showing through the light. She was actually smiling.

I shook hands with the obviously homosexual Christophe and immediately turned back to my girlfriend—ex-girlfriend. "My god, what are you doing here?!" I asked, still stunned.

"We thought we'd surprise you! Besides, Christophe is a big hockey fan." Surprise! That even had to be an understatement as I would probably rather use my own term, 'utter flabbergastation.' That better describes it. "We've been planning this since last weekend so we called the box office ahead of time for tickets. Good thing too, huh?"

"Umm-yeah…yeah, good thing."

"Do you have to go?" asked Amy, eyeing my teammates and

coaches loading on to the bus. "It's ok if you do, no big deal. We just wanted to say—"

"Hold on," I interrupted and focused on Christophe's uninterested face. "Can you give us a minute?" He backed away when Amy's head nodded in agreement, briskly walking back up the sidewalk en route to their parked vehicle. I caught the attention of Richard Hunt, seventy feet away in the parking lot, and held my pointer finger up high to say, "I'll be there in one minute." The equipment being packed into the underneath compartments bought me some time. "Amy, I miss you," I spat out, not looking at her directly.

"We have to talk some time."

Sigh. "I know." I've wanted to talk since December but she wasn't ready. "How come you haven't returned my calls?"

Amy released a cloud of steam-covered breath with a somewhat disgusted look upon her face. "Now isn't the time for that."

"Callie, let's go!" hollered Ridley from the steps of the bus while the last few bags were tossed underneath. I again raised my finger in their direction.

"Stay with us tonight," I articulated to my ex. "I'll talk with the coach to let you into the gym. I can probably get you tickets for tomorrow too."

"Dave, you know I can't do that, don't be ridiculous. Christophe and I have to get back to school."

"Yeah...yeah, I know. It was worth a shot, right?"

This cracked a chuckle from the girl pictured in my dreams as she shook her head left to right. "It's good to know you'll never change."

"Hurry up Callie, we're going to leave without you!"

"I'll be there in one second, hang on!"

Amy, beginning to lightly shiver from the cold, ordered me to join the team and promised that she'd speak to me later regarding our issues. It severely pained me to part ways at that moment, bringing up hurtful memories of Christmas evening and the agonizing two months that followed. At least this time, Amy swore we'd talk later.

"Call me this week if I don't first," remarked I before leaving her to drive the two hours back to Bowling Green. "Thank you so much for coming." I delivered a mighty uncomfortable hug to the beautiful girl (my body tingling the entire time) as she leaned her face up to my left cheek and planted the lightest, softest, fastest kiss right square in the center. She spoke nothing following the peck, but instead turned towards her particular parking lot, half-jogging to reach the Escort.

"Callie!"

"Coming!" I dashed at full speed, gym bag flapping back and forth against my leg, down the concrete stairs and across the deserted parking lot to the running bus. "HA haaaaah! Yes siree!" I screamed like a retarded idiot, exhaling all emotion. "Yes yes yes! Woooo hah! Yeah!" My echo was heard all through Columbus.

*****

The Buckeyes from Ohio State weren't very forgiving on us the following night, establishing a physical presence from the get-go and never letting up. Avulette's top line, full of seniors (and potential NHLers), didn't perform to their capacity on Friday night and in turn, were matched up with Alex, Michael and I the next evening while our tops faced off against OSU's second unit. Maybe it took them a full game, but the opposition's line full of veterans clicked on Saturday, manhandling us in every facet. It seemed every time our forwards found a glimmer of daylight, it was blocked immediately by an incredibly suffocating defense. I doubt a shot off my stick even found its way to the goaltender during the entire sixty minutes but thankfully, our line didn't allow a conflicting goal either.

The six hundred Michigan fans (exceeding the previous night's total) went home disappointed from the capital of Ohio, as their favorite team was actually in the game with ten minutes to play. We, unfortunately, just couldn't find a way to pull it off. One of OSU's hulking defensemen, Darren Bellows, netted an overwhelming slap shot goal at the 9:45 mark, giving his team a 3-1 advantage. State skated on to a 3-goal victory, maintaining the all-important seven-point lead on us in the competitive division.

Buckeye fans taunted our team and followers throughout the

weekend's games with such chants as "Sieve!" for the visiting goalie and their rendition of the notable song; "Sha na naaa na, na na naaa na, hey hey hey, you suck!" Clever, I'll admit. It made it difficult for any team to waltz in, expecting to stay focused and retain concentration once it had been rattled. During the latter of the weekend's matches, I suffered through an "individual player chant" where noisy students would monotonously sing, "Heeeeeeey, hey fourteen...I wanna know-woe-woe, why you suck so much!" to the tune of "Hey Baby." Punishing. It sounded like an intoxicated crowd singing along at a Bob Dylan concert. Ten wouldn't have been too bad, even twenty, but hundreds of mouths moving in unison to the same lyrics hurt. Prior to our first road game of the season (way back on October 19th, emerging victorious at St. Cloud, Minnesota), Trodeau warned us of unruly fans and measures to go about erasing their presence. It hadn't bothered me until the most recent game at OSU where even though fourteen wasn't the only number hollered, I took it to heart (something an athlete should NEVER do).

There was once a time, before bearing the yellow and blue, that I too had my place in the stands, joining my fellow fans in taunting any challenger of Michigan's. My father and I had belonged to the Dekers Blue Line Club (pronounced Deke-rs), the famed and most notable Wolverine booster group ever to exist. Its purpose was not only to support the program rich in tradition, but also to promote amateur hockey in the lakes area and establish a good foundation in the local high schools (which at the time involved me at Fenton's finest). Every athlete and hockey admirer in Michigan was familiar with the Dekers from the time of Vic Heyliger in 1962 to the present and its continually growing membership. They stood out at each hockey game, home and away, dressed in their "DekerWear" (which for my tenure in the organization consisted of lemon yellow t-shirts for the lot) while much like the Buckeye faithful, we mocked the enemy's goalie, attempting to disrupt his concentration. Only now did I realize how disturbing it truly was to the humans on the ice. And they were human, with real feelings.

The Blue Line Club has funded the school's championship trophies over the 41 years of its existence, along with rings for graduating seniors, exercise equipment for the ice arena from 50 / 50 raffles, picnics and other such events. In turn, we got priority tickets to every UM game we chose. The Deker Blue Like Club Scholarship had been created from the group's money too as during my high school graduation ceremony, I was announced one of the lucky recipients. I couldn't argue with five hundred bonus dollars towards my only choice college.

The three years of being a Deker were some of the best and most entertaining in my life. My father and I must have seen approximately thirty games in that span, including two away games in East Landing and Lake Superior. I remember that Michigan-Michigan State game distinctly, for it was the first time I ever routed against the home team in a foreign arena. My dad (who looked quite ridiculous in that fluorescent yellow shirt) and I were situated behind the visiting goal in the Munn Arena with our five hundred allies going against the over five thousand Spartan large. We were anything but subdued. Whether five, five hundred, or five thousand, the contingent of Dekers spent those three hours hooting, hollering and stomping our feet in support of the Wolverines while chanting back at the annoyed home crowd.

The game itself was surely memorable; an overtime tally off the stick of Mike Comrie (now a star for the Edmonton Oilers) gave us a 4-3 triumph that late February evening and a national ranking of number one. I envied and admired those 1998-99' athletes from Comrie to Josh Langfeld to Jeff Jillson to net minder Josh Blackburn—even to head coach Jerry Trodeau. All now posed in portraits, lining the interior walls of the Yost with their respective statistics in plaques underneath. Comrie was one of the best to ever wear the uniform. As Dad and I watched the young stud deke out State's goalie from beside the net, we threw up our hands in exuberance and high five'd each other (along with the crazy club members). "Great Goal!" I remember Dad saying, "What a big win! You like that stuff, don't you State?" He was humorously out of control. I never exactly knew if my father really did love the Wolverines or if he just acted that way for my benefit. You know, to please me. I'll never forget that energized high five though; it's plenty difficult to describe just how it exactly affected me. I will tell you this though; running these images through the VCR of my brain made me sorry for storming out of the house last Sunday. It at least deserved an apologetic call. For after all, the two of us were once bonded together during the winter's college hockey season as part of the Blue Line Club. Once a Deker, always a Deker.

15

So I purchased Amy a necklace. A quite nice one too, ½ ct. diamond heart pendant, thirty-four round diamonds set in 10 karats of gold. I even got a few links taken out to fit her neck perfectly. Retailed at $400, I paid one hundred under the stock price. And I couldn't feel guiltier spending it.

Three hundred dollars of steaming, stolen money from a man who had laid all of his deepest trust in me! When slapping those fifteen bills onto the counter, I found it impossible to match eyesight with the curious cashier. Yes, I know—how could anyone distinguish regular cash from that which was hot? Answer being, they can't. I was perfectly aware of this at the counter, but my clammy palms wouldn't cease perspiration and my heart wanted to break restraint from my chest. The checkout was more nail-biting than my first hockey game! Unfortunately, everything went fine as I exited the store with the expensive necklace in its jewelry case. Now that I had completed the hardest task, my genius plan would have to be followed to the finish.

Nobody knew of this (especially my parents, who in a matter of hours would receive that call of apology), except me. I had the conflict, I derived the plan, and I'll execute the plan, alone. God forbid an outside party should know; they'd label me crazy and the likelihood of the whole shebang going to hell would increase. All judgments and second-guessing would come straight from the source.

Later that same afternoon, I stopped at CVS for a mushy greeting card before packaging up the two items and sending them off to

Amy's dormitory address in Bowling Green, Ohio. Now I would have to sit back and wait. Wait for a response I had been dreaming of from that frigid January afternoon on the park bench. I just wished for my girlfriend back. Friday's escapade surely didn't help the emotional state, seeing Amy at her finest, wondering if she felt the same as myself. Why else would she forfeit University Party Night to drive an astounding two hours (plus the return trip) to watch a sport that most women don't even enjoy? And that kiss! Sweet nectar of life! Had I expected her pouched lips touching my skin, I would have gone for the gusto, hit the homerun, lit up the scoreboard, collected the marbles—you understand—I would have turned my head to intercept the kiss with lips of my own. That would have gotten things really rocking.

Monday passed, Tuesday as well, until Wednesday's date flashed on my computer. The waiting game was driving me into a state of lunacy. You know I would have presented Ms. Lewis with her present in person had I not been such a coward at the present date. Fear of rejection, I guess you could say, a feeling I was new to experience. So being the newest Loser Hall Of Fame's inductee, I kept the phone line available and had an instant messenger service signed on to my computer round-the-clock (college Ethernet T-1 lines are simply the greatest). Knowing Amy, and women for that matter, she would contact me as soon as the jewelry arrived in her mailroom. How I wish I wasn't so chickenshit.

From five o'clock until twenty minutes past, I took a fast bathroom break and visited with Eric Lessard (who lived in the same building, two floors above Adley and I). The both of us had two rare days off from hockey practice and found ourselves at a loss for entertainment. Fancy that. When returning to the hole-in-the-wall, my roommate wheeled around in his chair from his segregated side of the room to announce the big news.

"Your girlfriend called."

Score! "She called when I was out? What did she say? Anything about the jewelry?"

"She left no message, just to ring her back." Adley swiveled back to his workstation in order to engulf himself back in a web page.

"Was she at school?"

My roomy shrugged his shoulders. "How should I know?" Worthless hunk of junk!

"I thought she might have mentioned it. Amy goes to Bowling Green for future reference."

"Amy?" asked my confused roommate. "No, that wasn't who called. It was the girl that was here a couple weeks ago...Tamara or something."

"Shit, Tanya."

"Yeah, that's it. She is your girlfriend, right?" Cynically, I laughed but didn't answer. Of course she's my girlfriend, in her fantasy world of unicorns, fairies, airborne pigs on nudity on first dates. Her mind was so warped that she most likely referred to ten guys as her boyfriends. Basically, anyone stupid enough to be lured into bed with the mess herself! A cute mess but a mess nonetheless. "A mess nonetheless is what I address to confess," would say Dr. Seuss, regarding the situation.

I continued to wait and wait and wait. Wednesday night had passed, as did Thursday like molasses, until the end of a long week had arrived. Another hockey weekend was looming; a home-and-home series would be in store two consecutive nights against Western Michigan. Game time was slated for seven thirty and Trodeau, being Trodeau, wanted his men dressed at a quarter to six. His orders allowed me only ten fast minutes in the dormitory room following my excursion to Market Basket for groceries before hitching a ride with Sean to the rink. Entering the hole-in-the-wall, I lobbed the bags of food into my armoire and immediately ran to the computer without extricating my jacket. Sitting down would eat up too much valuable time so I bent across the back of the chair and clicked the mouse to view my e-mail page. There, staring at me from the inbox, sat the response.

Trying to conceal any sort of expression, I exhaled large and said, "Here it is."

TO: Dcalvetto@hotmail.com
Subject: (No Subject)

Hello David,

I can't accept this gift. Don't get me wrong, the necklace is beautiful but it's far too expensive and I don't deserve it. You can't do this David. You can't spend loads of money on me in a plea to get back together because it's not going to happen. I love you, I'll always love you but it isn't going to work anymore, we're two completely different people now.

It would mean a lot to me to remain friends—I couldn't envision my life without you in it. I hope you can understand that. The necklace is being mailed back to your school address. I'm sorry.

—Amy

Sean Collins had walked in at the wrong time. Two ruled notebooks, once sitting peacefully upon my desk, whipped across the small room, knocking the opposite wall and nearly nicking the big six footer in the doorway. I hung my head and violently punched the desktop in a downward motion. Bad move.

"Did I ah…miss something?" asked a worried Sean.

"Oh no," I answered, beginning to get quite sarcastic. "Just me getting screwed over again. That contradicting bitch, what does that even mean, 'I couldn't envision my life without you in it?'" My rant grew more boisterous with every syllable. "That girl doesn't know what the hell she wants!"

"Dude," butted in Collins. "What's going on?"

I just continued with, "She didn't have the decency to call! What a waste! What a damn waste!" Again, I took out anger on the desk. "All that for nothing!" Thankfully, Adley wasn't present to witness the eruption of Mount Calvetto, as he'd probably run scared. Instead, my big, bruising friend would have to control the volcano.

"Whoa! For Christ's sake Callie, relax…get a grip!" My blood boiled as I did try to 'get a grip' by freezing my body in place, making it shake wildly.

"Errrrr," I let loose between my gritted teeth (they pressed against each other so hard, I thought they would shatter). Finally, I spoke to Sean who appeared to be surprisingly terrified. "Women! I hate women. They hold you hostage, make you love them and then fuck you over. They completely fuck you over! Just tell me 'why'? Why does the entire species feel the need to screw me, man? Why?" Not able to keep my cool, I wanted to lash out and destroy everything in sight.

"What happened man? I've never seen you like this before."

"Well, I've never felt like this." A deep breath was released from my cheeks and seeped through my teeth's gaps. "Do you remember last Friday when Amy came to Columbus and kissed me after our game?" Sean nodded slowly. "It meant nothing. The girl wants nothing to do with me."

Collins seemed unsure of what to say. I'm positive that girls have never pulled this selfish act on him. "Hey I'm sorry guy." Pause. "We'll make sure to find you somebody—"

"I don't want anybody else," I retorted with a nasty tone (I was far past sick of people telling me that).

"Well, try to put the situation behind you man, I'm sure it must be difficult." My friend (still stationed in the doorway for fear of getting near the ticking time bomb) peered at his watch. "Come on, we have to be down there in five minutes...you are still coming, right?"

"Sure, why not? Maybe I can kill somebody."

"There you go!"

I flicked the power switch located on my computer's tower (no further need for e-mail) and collected my pre-packed equipment. A hugely important hockey game was barreling down on us and did I care? No. I was too emotionally distraught to give my best athletic ability for the night. If Trodeau knew what was best, he'd bench me.

"Alright, let's go," I announced heatedly.

"Cheer up brother, you'll be fine once we win. We'll go party-hunting later."

*****

"Welcome to the jungle, we've got fun and games, we got everything you want, blah blah blah blah blaaah." Oh, how I abhorred that song. Every game it's the same tedious program: "Please welcome your two thousand and three Michigan Wolverines."

We file through the tunnel to thunderous applause until all blades hit the ice. And then: "Welcome to the jungle, we've got fun and games…" By the midpoint in the extensive season, one would be immune to the outdated rock anthem, hearing not what pumped through the poorly managed sound system. Tonight, *everything* would bother me. From the music to the bright lights (I was forced to squint from the floods penetrating through my eyelids) to the nasty glares delivered by the Western Michigan thugs. If intimidation was the ultimate goal, then they had failed. Skating in wide pre-game circles around our given zone, I flashed cynical giggles whenever converging with a rival player. What were they trying to prove? Eighth place in the conference certain provides no intimidation factor for me.

I was becoming far too accustomed to the intense atmosphere of the Yost (along with additional college hockey arenas in our immediate area). Although my first year wasn't yet complete, nothing shocked me anymore; the stadium would be filled, night in and night out, students and Dekers would occasionally dip body parts in paint, we constantly ran the invariable warm-up drills—same stuff, different night is what it all boiled down to. The only unusual detail was the bunch of feisty butterflies residing in the pit of my stomach during every home game. It was that nervously unsure feeling; the kind children get on their first day of school. You know the one I'm talking about. Even after turning in my first few shifts, the bothersome nerves would cease to subside; actually, not until the clock reached straight zeros and we were back relaxing in the showers. Few professional hockey players have explained that throughout their illustrious careers, the butterfly aspect remains with them until the very end. How can one experience uncertainty in his twenty-something'th year of employment? The average dimwit would expect him to be comfortable in his usual surroundings by the time of retirement. Just my two cents!

The puck was released from the head referee's grip while I irregularly looked on from my bench spot. You've all heard the phrase, "I was there but I really wasn't." Well, I was physically accounted for in the arena but my mind was far from the sport at hand as could be. I wasn't even watching a hockey game, but rather a huge blur of white and animate colors. It resembles a—

My helmet slid down over my face from an Alex Hutchinson slap off the top. "Wake up," he ordered softly enough for the coaches not to hear.

"I'm awake."

The play was pushed into our zone, carried by one opponent gliding across the blue line to set up a formation offense in front of our bench.

"Pick him up Derek (Strickland)!" yelled Trodeau, banging our eardrums. The freshman winger botched the move as a clean shot on goal was taken, but missed wide left. "Behind the net!" Our players were outraced to the puck again by a small, wiry Bronco forward (who couldn't have topped six feet on stilts) wearing the number twenty-nine in brown. He gathered in the corner, circled around while cradling the puck, deked out an embarrassed Jeff Thomas going for the steal, and zinged a crisp pass out to the far face-off circle. Strick nearly tipped the pass but over skated it as another wrist shot was taken. "Defense defense defense!" Hooden continued to bail us out during the miserable shift, making a kick save on the point-blank shot. "Get me somebody who can play!" screamed the aggravated coach only three minutes and change into the divisional contest. "Line Three! Change it up!" While the moving puck skidded untouched across the neutral zone, my mates and I leapt over the two-foot boards, landing in precision on the wet, slippery ice surface. "Spread out!" The Broncos opted to remain with their current line, which had spent the previous sixty seconds peppering our poor goalie. What an onerous load to wear on Scott's shoulders.

Stutzel immediately gained control of the puck at center ice, slapping a short pass from the head of his stick to mine, moving down the right wing boards. Sensing no attack from our offense, I tipped the rubber circle onto my stick in a fancy forty-five degree angle and heaved it deep into their corner, forcing the idle goaltender to lazily gather.

"Callie, hold on to the puck!" coached Trodeau loud and clear from his commanding post. 'Why don't you get out here and do it old man? Every play in hockey consists of a split-second decision where it is only human to occasionally pick the wrong one. So shut your hypocritical mouth up!' Lousy coaches, what are they good for?

The Broncos (from the University of Western Michigan) changed up their defensive pairing on the dump in, sending in two undersized juniors to compliment the tired forwards. The diminutive number twenty-nine crossed behind his net, waited for the new defense to take position and started up ice while showboating some fancy stick-handling moves. Meanwhile, I skated backwards (a technique much more difficult than it appears) from the blue line out past center ice to halt the oncoming rush.

"Let's go Mi-chi-gan," chanted the Dekers to the pattering 'clap clap clap-clap clap' of their hands.

"Stop them defense! Get back!"

I once again squinted from the unnecessarily penetrating light rays, which on this particular night were burning my retinas; and wouldn't you know it, I lost track of the play. When my vision came to, Shorty had trickled past me and fed the puck to a streaking teammate's stick.

"Get your head in the game Callie!"

"Let's go Mi-chi-gan!"

From behind, I horizontally jabbed my lumber into the small of Tiny's back before setting up the umbrella defense; Alex, Mike and I fanned out at the point with our two defensemen (Walsh and Kotti) acting as the handle to prevent shots from sneaking through. West Michigan's feisty forward, obviously upset with my horseplay, delivered a blow to the backside of my helmet when moving by. Oh, this weakling was asking for it—no, easy Calvetto. Keep it calm.

"Booo! Where's the call ref?" questioned the Club, up in arms (a valid point being as the rear of my head now stung).

Thankfully, no shots reached Hooden from the firing Bronco offense, as I was relieved of my mistake. Walsh cleared our zone, sending the puck all the way up the left wing boards for an icing whistle. Phew, a break in the action. After being on the ice for only eighty seconds of game time, I was entirely deflated. Winded! Spent! God, get me out of this dreaded arena.

My newest archenemy, number twenty-nine in the visiting jerseys, gave me quite the forearmed shove when crossing paths to our relevant benches. The cheap whack came to my shoulder blade, throwing my weight off-balance and onto one leg. The crowd hollered, the coach protested, my teammates ganged around, but the referees remained silent. "Easy Callie. He's not worth the trouble," I reminded myself as I silently took a seat on the bench.

Three more opening period shifts followed with nothing spectacular to show for. The game was much more physical than most, sparked by unwarranted jostling between the short, determined tormenter and I. This kid was getting on my nerves, so much so that I would picture his skinny face, full of week-old stubble, all the way through our tunnel and into the locker room—actually, I should say 'nearly' to our locker room. One scuffle had ceased and without warning, another began.

Smack! The bare hand of Gerry Walsh grabbed my left pectoral pad, making the noise against its plastic covering. My body was pulled backwards and spun around with Gerry's steaming angry face directed at mine.

"Hey, you better wake up out there!" yelled the senior captain, sprinkles of saliva flying every which way, "I'm tired of doing this by myself! Quit skating half-assed and do your job!" The remainder of the boys had stopped short before reaching the dressing room's door, all standing with that 'deer in the headlights' stunned look. To my surprise, the young but fearless Sean opened his mouth.

"Leave him alone Gerry, the kid is doing his best."

Walsh, now fuming, tightened his clutch on my pads. "His best? His best, you say?! Are you out of your mind Collins? The kid is standing around out there—he's going to lose us the game!" My heavily cushioned body was pinned against the hallway's brick wall courtesy of a vigorous shove by Gerry's strong hand. I still hadn't uttered a word.

The surrounding teammates (appalled at what they were witnessing) hollered in chorus but didn't interfere with the altercation. That is, all except for Sean. His colossal body came behind Captain's, throwing both massive tree arms around his neck and prying his grasp from me. Gerry nearly collapsed backwards under the force.

"What is your problem Collins?" interrogated everybody's 'favorite' Wolverine, who now had the look of insanity, standing between Sean and I. His arms were positioned above the chest, ready to fight whomever attacked first. And right on cue, Sean lunged for his abdomen when –

"Knock it off, all of you!" came booming from down the corridor. This was an order unlike I had ever heard, making every active body freeze up much like liquid does on a winter's day, including the antagonist himself. We stood immobile, resembling children in a principal's office. "Let's go, out of the hall! Now! I don't have time for this crap!"

I didn't know what was more embarrassing; being threatened by a guy who stands five inches shorter than I, or by a member of my own team. 'Playing the role of the classic piñata this evening...David Ernest Calvetto! Everybody step up and take your swings!' One more mental hit and I would be broken apart, letting the candy flow out.

"Thanks," I mentioned to my best friend Sean during the first period intermission. His hand batted in the air to signal, 'think nothing of it' from my neighboring locker. The whole situation sent him into a sour mood along with the rest, making for a silent, eerie and uncomfortable ten minutes between frames. Not even the coaching staff had words of wisdom to say. We sat mute, most covering our heads, before shipping back out for the second twenty minutes of play—something we should never have done.

The six thousand in attendance welcomed us back with open arms, oblivious to the inter-squad problems that arose directly beneath their feet, under the stands. I imagined the coaches would cover up the fiasco following the game. In any case, I would put any differences behind me for the remaining two hours, secluding myself in my own world and blocking the Gerry Walshs' that cluttered it up—as well as the Amy Lewis', the Tanya Aikens', the Steven Toscanos', even Mr. And Mrs. Calvetto who all seethed my anger on this particular night. However, everybody has a breaking point—and here came mine.

It wasn't the overactive Walsh, or the boisterous coach, but rather the meaningless five-foot-six midget who picked the wrong guy to jostle with. He was an annoying housefly, buzzing incessantly around the ears until your backhand finally connected with the little devil, sending him to a sudden death—and although relieved, you can't help but sympathize for the poor insect. Not much larger than the average fly, my shorter opponent wouldn't stop darting in and out of my vision line or quickly landing in spots where I couldn't smack him dead. But this little kid was worse than any bug. If a quarter were paid for every cheap shot (high stick, elbow or shoulder) to the mid-section, this kid would inherit a pocket full of change. I ignored his demeaning trash talking, shrugged off two trips (spilling me to the ice both times), and even failed to retaliate on a bump to the chin by Shorty's glove. Sadly, with our team down 2-1 and my young, energetic line on the ice, all hell broke loose.

Perhaps I should begin by saying the referees unfairly ejected me from the game. So for the red-shirted freshman record second time, I took that long head-down walk from the ice level to our locker room, accompanied by a Yost security guard and a mix of cheers and jeers raining down from the paid audience. The dressing room scene was one which will never be forgotten, but let me first explain how it all came about.

The visiting team's coach had obviously sensed his five-foot-sixer wearing me down, so naturally, whenever our third line was called upon, his countered. The squabble occurred after a whistle (blown for offside), as once again the feeble forward performed his best deaf impersonation by claiming he hadn't heard the tweet. That's when the unannounced and painful check to my ribs came. "Oomph," escaped from my mouth as my breath was momentarily taken away. Without spending a much-needed second to calm and regain composure, I let my temper invade, racing after the hooligan and grabbing his collar, much as Gerry did to me. My clenched fist rose at the once-intimidating opponent, who now stood defenseless and panic-stricken, realizing it was more than just a game now. His wide eyes stared in fear at my oncoming wrath. Then flashbacks. I pictured the hefty, drunken galoot from that one dreary night on campus, his eyes rolling back in his head when anticipating a punch. "I'm not the fighting type," is what covered me then. However, now, everything that was once dubbed wrong seemed right. I hurled my closed fist directly at the shrimp's right cheek, stinging the knuckles instantly, and delivered two more punches to his temple before being restrained. How worked up was I? Ask me what teammates curtailed me and I honestly couldn't answer. Moreover, I was fully off the ice and halfway down the hall when my penalty (and ejection) was announced over the loudspeaker. I had snapped.

Now, back to the locker room. Not surprisingly, my helmet was unstrapped and launched across the open room before I could settle myself down. And when the calming did hit, it wasn't a pretty sight—because that's when it happened folks; my body collapsed like a rag doll against the carpeted floor as I covered my head with both hands...and openly cried.

16

The morning after, I laid underneath my heavy comforter and thought of Dad. "Before you know it, this new temper will get your butt kicked off the team so fast, you won't know it happened. What a waste of talent that'd be. Unbelievable." Thankfully, I would retain a roster spot, but it took a thirty-minute conference with Trodeau and a member of the NCAA Rules Committee to do so. The college hockey rulebook states that two on-ice fistfights in a matter of one season results in an automatic suspension for the remainder of that year.

Since this was technically my first scuffle, the board director went lenient on me as he also got some persuasion from the coach, backing my side. That, I didn't expect.

Let's face it; I was a crook, a cheat, a liar, a bully—possibly more—and it all knocked me unconscious like a ton of bricks in that empty locker room. Staring at the dormitory's ceiling tiles early the next morning (while Adley snored away like a hacksaw), I continually asked myself: *How did I let this happen?* How did little innocent Davie Calvetto become a public enemy? Was it over a girl? Over a game? Couldn't handle the pressure or being in the media spotlight? I searched and searched but couldn't uncover the answers to these questions. I did know this though; from the present day of February 24th forward, I would have to be courageous and face my problems. There would be no more turning of the cheek and watching as matters grew out of control, all the while waiting for a suitable resolution to appear. Unfortunately, life doesn't work that way.

*****

The front door to our beautiful woods-hidden house eased open with my mother, dressed in leisurely weekend sweats, greeting me across the archway. She failed to provide her normal 'good-to-see-you-son smile' but instead, gave an uneasy, almost sympathetic curl of the upper lip, exposing the two dimples, more as if to say, 'I miss my former son, but welcome home.' My mother also didn't immediately hug me at the doorway—no, I hugged her first. I desired the safety of maternal arms holding me tight, protecting me from all evil.

"What's happened Dave?"

"I don't know, Mom. It all just fell apart."

The coach and I agreed it best for me to sit out the evening's game at Western Michigan. 'Personal Reasons,' would be listed beside my name on the team's roster card. Mr. Trodeau was far more understanding than I could have imaged during our mid-morning meeting in the school's athletic department. Not once did he raise his voice or lose his cool, collective manners. After the Rules Committee member had vacated the office, my coach took a minute to speak to me personally.

"Dave, I've noticed incredible talent in you from the first tryout. You've got a gift—a very rare gift—and the potential to become one of the league's best someday. But here's the catch, please...please talk to one of us if your personal issues are becoming too much—you know my office door is open and I'm always willing to help. Or if I can't, believe me I will find somebody who will." The coach tipped back in his expensive leather chair, scratched his chin and began to recite an old story—obviously, not the first time it was told. "You know Callie, I was a lot like you in college (You!? Nah!). Shy kid, hard worker, always wanting to be the absolute best—I did skate three years for Michigan you know. Well, after leading the team in scoring my junior year, a freak accident finished me off the following season. Remember, heavy pads weren't around in those days. Anyway, during the final period of one game, my feet came out from under me and I slid at full speed into the opposite team's goal, with their goalie collapsing on top. The blade of his skate dug right into my forearm—all the way down to the bone. Heck, he couldn't feel worse about it. But that incident was the beginning of the end, Callie, I never returned that season—couldn't stickhandle or shoot anymore. Once the professional clubs dropped me from consideration, I gave up. Can you even fathom that? Here I was, a twenty-one-year-old kid destined to reach the top when my dream abruptly ended." Sigh. "It was all over."

Through his roundabout way, I think I understood the coach's moral to this story. The sad truth is, we never know exactly what the future brings—so why not make the best of the present day? Trodeau did. Although he never made the big show, his legacy remained in the halls of the Yost and the respect for him contained no boundaries.

I parted the lengthy hug from my mother and staggered into the house, my feet dragging against the carpet. The spacious living room provided a great welcome sight; a place of security which I so badly desired. My head pounded from its stuffiness, eyes and ears feeling like 10-ton anvils, but as I released my suitcase on the landing, I gazed around and smiled. Home.

"Oh, it's you," grunted a voice from the staircase. "I was having a good weekend too."

"Mike, would you shut up?"

"Oh great, here we go again—Mom, I'm leaving!" My aggravating brother began to retrace his steps and stamped back up the stairs to his bedroom.

"Wait," I called in his direction. "Wait, I'm sorry." Mike ascended two steps and halted suddenly, giving me a wide-eyed look of confusion. "I didn't mean it like that, can you forgive me?"

Astonishment inhabited the youngster. "What?"

"I've been a real jerk lately and I'm sorry. Things just blew up in my face last night. Forgive me?"

My brother couldn't uncover the correct words to say. He simply stood there, halfway up the staircase, dumbfounded at what seemed a genuinely sincere apology. "Who are you and what have you done with David?"I expected him to ask in a smart-alecky tone. That's what Mikey did best. Instead, the high-schooler opened his mouth and muttered, "Yeah sure, whatever. It's fine."

My mother stood silently smiling at her two boys, having one of those gratifying moments where teaching the kids manners (among other ways of life) had once again paid off. I can't exactly describe the feeling considering my parental days would come far from the present. However, looking at that all too familiar grin, I knew her maternal skills accounted for it. The whole scene reminded me of a sappy movie (probably one Amy dragged me to) where throughout the mother's battle with her son or daughter, everything comes full circle in the end making for that cinematic moment which sent tears to the audience. Except me of course! Of course. No way am I the sappy type. Not me! Nah!

Mom waited for Mikey to trudge upstairs before pouring out her emotions at me.

"You're such a good kid Davie, don't let anyone convince you otherwise."

"I do what I can."

It took me roughly eleven and a half minutes from the time I entered through the front door until I was buried underneath the covers in my queen-sized bed. That had to be a record. The previous night's experience had completely wiped my energy away; I felt like a runner after finishing his first marathon. All I wished was to sleep it off, to erase the recent memory that invaded my head. To my surprise, I did sleep through the afternoon...and dreamt about nothing.

March 2003

17

Hutch, Stutz, Collins, JT, Hoover, Walshy, Strick, Dee, the Frenchman, King Marcus, Callie; quite an odd group to make for a winning combination. We fought, we partied, we disobeyed orders, but we never slacked. And we won games.

"Ha ha, I can't believe Sean and I were caught upstairs," I reminisced to myself with a deep-bellied laugh while sitting Indian style on the wooden bench. "What the hell were we thinking?"

Today's drawing wasn't of the ordinary college scenery that occupied twenty-one pages of my designated notebook. No, today I would sketch caricatures of all my hockey pals with a large bubbled headline on top of the page reading: "Dekers Blue Line Club 2002-2003." Once a Deker, always a Deker. My crowded notebook page featured the penciled outline of Sean, big and muscular, bench-pressing a load of weights, the Hoover standing poised in front of a hand-drawn goal, Alex and Michael at opposite ends of the page (signifying my two line mates) with both sketched sticks facing inward, and finally our coach (standing twice the size of any other person on the page) in the center, both hands cupped against the side of his mouth in his customary hollering motion. Nowhere on the sheet, not even hidden away in a corner, could you find a picture of Amy. Or Tanya. Not to say I seriously disliked either one but I was finished causing more problems than were needed. "No girls," I mumbled under my breath. "For a long, long time." Taking a quick break from my sketch to gather my vast thoughts, I reconsidered and said, "Well, at least until the season is over." No more distractions. No more worrying. No more—

"Excuse me," came a female voice approaching from my right. "Are you Dave Calvetto?" The girl, who I estimated to be a good six inches shorter than I, stood unaccompanied with long black hair blowing in the wind, a button-down cotton jacket covering her upper body and tight blue jeans. She had a cute face—one of those where makeup wasn't even needed to enhance her image—and I noticed this right away.

"Yeah. Yeah, that's me," I responded to the stranger while slapping my notebook closed. Drawing random scenes or people wasn't exactly something I cared to share.

"I thought so! My name is Amanda," introduced the girl, extending her small hand out to meet mine. "I see you around campus all the time. We're in the same psychology class." Considering it was a special occasion when I actually attended that class, I never noticed Amanda in the lecture hall. Amazing that on one of those rare days, she spotted me.

I politely shook the young girl's hand and said, "It's nice to meet you Amanda."

"Feel free to call me Mandie, all of my friends do."

"Okay Mandie, it's nice to meet you," I repeated, unable to find another sentence. What did she expect? I knew absolutely nothing about this dark-haired girl other than the fact she was outspoken and had a nice face (for most guys, that was enough!).

"I hear you're an excellent hockey player. I'd go to the games but I'm busy most weekends with the student union." Why was she still talking?

"I wouldn't consider myself *excellent* (especially after inciting a riot on the ice). I'm only a first-year player."

Mandie now stepped forward and leaned against the bench's arm. She tossed her blowing hair aside like all the stereotypical valley girls do. "Well, you make the newspaper all the time so you *must* be good. Don't laugh, I'm serious!" Mandie could sense the conversation tumbling downhill. "I have to get to class, it was very nice to meet you," she articulated with a fake smile.

"I'll see you in class." Something about that smile hit me in a strange way. It was reminiscent of the expression girl's give when being shot down by their longtime admirer. The whole "fuck you for making me like you" look. Mandie walked, green backpack strapped over both shoulders, away from me towards the campus pond and hooked a left onto the dirt path.

"Hey!" I hollered in her direction after shoving my artist's notebook deep into my bag. I leapt off the bench to chase the girl down. "Hey Mandie!" She halted and spun around in confusion, looking surprised to hear her own name. What it was that hit me then, I was unsure of, but when reaching the candid female I asked, "Can I have your number? Maybe I can call you sometime."

No girls until the season was over—that strategy crashed and burned. How about no girl until the end of the afternoon? Or the hour? Or the minute? Easier said than done I suppose.

Over the coming days and weeks, I would rise from bed and attend my 9:30 psych class more frequently, sometime sitting alongside Mandie to help each other study. She turned out to be a very cool person—Vice President of the student union, a member of the distinguished honor's program, long time jazz dancer and much more for me to soon discover. Was she Amy Lewis? No. Never would be. However, I enjoyed her company and that was what I really needed at the current time. In addition, she certainly wasn't the worst looking girl across campus.

One early morning (early according the college students—not for me anymore), while uncomfortably sitting in a non-padded lecture hall chair, I was called upon by Professor Sedgwick in psychology. She had the roster of all one hundred and fifteen students beside her lecture notes and regularly picked a random name to keep us all awake. This day, her wandering pointer finger had landed on Calvetto.

Towards the beginning of our discussion on sleeping behaviors, the female professor asked: "Mr. Calvetto, what percent of sleep do newborn's spend dreaming?"

Mandie whispered the answer before I stood up and recited "Eighty percent professor."

"Very good." I softly thanked the girl dressed in red and plopped down in the uncomfortable seat. "Whoa, I'm not done with you yet," spoke Mrs. Sedgwick clearly through her clipped microphone. The two classroom speakers amplified her voice for everyone to hear. "Stand back up, Mr. Calvetto. Thank you. If you all remember from Monday's lecture, we discussed the difference between manifest, latent and lucid dreams. Manifest are the normal dreams or nightmares that you experience every night due to what we remember or what's fresh in our minds." The professor paused to swallow and adjust the microphone on her lapel. "Mr. Calvetto, can you tell the class what *latent* dreams are and why we have them?" The entire class shifted their weight to face the standing me in the back right corner of the auditorium. Talk about being singled out; at 9:30 no less.

"Well," I began apprehensively from the one hundred pairs of staring eyes (you think I'd be used to the anxiety by now). "Latent dreams deal with our unconscious thoughts and wishes that umm…need a great deal of thought before they are understood. I believe they're mostly triggered by our innermost desires, which may not even be realized at times. For example…if you have a crush or obsession with a member of the opposite sex, they may be recurring throughout many of your dreams. Whether they play an active role in the dream or not, the important part is they're present. This person, male or female, represents your wish or desire that most often is unattainable. So basically, it's proven that we have latent dreams to stay sane and they're good indicators of what is on our minds."

Sedgwick seemed appalled at my elaborate response, as she stood speechless for five long seconds. I feared I had said too much. Even Amanda had a bewildered look upon her early-morning face.

"*That's* a good answer," remarked our professor for the entire classroom to hear. "Very good. You may have a seat."

Phew. Luckily, this was the one section I had read up on before coming to class. I hope Professor Sedgwick now found me halfway intelligent.

"Wow!" uttered Mandie softly into my ear. "Did you have some sort of personal experience with this?"

"I guess you could say that."

18

The CCHA playoffs lasted one enormously long, tiring week. The postseason began on a Thursday night, March the 17th, with us as the number two seed in the division hosting Notre Dame in a best of three series. For the first time in five weeks, our entire squad was healthy; Vitek had fully recovered from the nagging wrist injury, Strick returned after two missed games due to a small foot problem, and me...well, I was feeling better. Before our final regular season contest, I stated a public apology to my teammates in hopes for forgiveness—it was the right thing to do. So by the 17th, my "personal issues" were far behind us as we fought for the CCHA championship.

Friday and Saturday brought lopsided wins in our favor in the form of 5-1 and 6-2, eliminating the Fighting Irish and pushing us on to the semifinals. The following Wednesday, our bus departed for Joe Louis Arena in the big city, which for fifteen consecutive years had housed the CCHA's final four. For the semifinal game against Michigan State, we were assigned the home locker room; that which the Detroit Red Wings themselves used. The names of Yzerman, Federov, Lidstrom, Shanahan and more were printed above each individual wooden locker in red and white, giving me the serious shivers. The manager's office sat twenty feet down the extended hallway from the square-shaped locker room, where famed coach Scotty Bowman once did business. The whole area reeked of tradition and legends of the past (as well as the present). For one night, I felt on top of the world.

Maybe it was the adrenaline and simply the fact I used and dressed in front of Chris Chelios' locker (a boyhood hero of mine) but I tore up the Joe Louis ice that evening with two huge goals and two assists, both to my line mate Alex. Overall, I factored into four of the team's six tallies, en route to a 6-2 victory, and got voted the number two star of the game (even though Scott Hooden let in two, he stopped a career-high forty-six shots making him deserving of the top honors). When the three stars were announced following the conclusion of the game, I erupted of the bench and onto the ice in jubilation, skating in a large donut to acknowledge my star-worthy performance while waving my arms in the air to our supportive Wolverine faithful. The Blue Line Club, sitting behind the goal, went wild for their old member, son and friend. Once a Deker, always a Deker. The Club was now praising *me*.

"You were the number one star in my mind!" exclaimed the Hoover as I came off the ice into the tunnel. He stood there, goalie equipment still fully on (minus the mask) awaiting his celebratory circle amidst the cheers from the student body.

"Thanks man," I answered, patting my friend on the shoulder.

*****

The top two seeds survived the challenge and pushed through to the championship game. Number one Ohio State versus number two Michigan. The winner would earn a berth to the 16-team NCAA playoffs while the loser would most likely go home. As the history books explain, it would be one match for all the marbles. And it would undoubtedly be "The Clash of the Titans."

Owning the coveted top spot, Ohio State was granted the Red Wing locker room while we took the less luxurious of the two. There were no world-renowned names above our lockers or a famed coach's quarter down the hall but NHL superstars had definitely began and ended key games in this very room. If nothing else, it was a sure upgrade from the decrepit Yost. Besides, all twenty-five Michigan players and coaches were too excited / nervous / focused to care. I had sat crossed-legged on the floor to practice meditation for five minutes before lacing up the skates and connecting the Cooper-brand pads. The expected crowd was 16,000.

Both teams took the saturated ice at the exact second prior to face-off. As I followed my teammates through Joe Louis' tunnel (much wider and brighter than ours), the tedious Guns N' Roses guitar riff could be heard filling the immense stadium. No, god no. Anything but that! I don't know if I could take "Welcome To The Jungle" one more time. The game was held in a neutral arena and STILL, the overplayed song managed to find it's way into the thumping speakers. All that stuff I said about jacking us up before a game—well, forget it.

The subconscious crowd (split 50 / 50 between Buckeye and Wolverine followers) continued to rock and sing along, probably not even realizing what song was playing. I'll refrain from describing the remainder of the pre-game festivities—you can probably visualize it by now. It was becoming common nature to me. One thing I *would* like to mention was that positioned on the Michigan side of the arena stood my parents, brother and grandfather (who traveled down from Palms Point to Detroit early that morning). Grandpa, all 77 years of him, cheered passionately for his grandson's team, waving a hilarious-looking blue and yellow pom-pom in the air. You're never too old to act like a kid.

The game began with a stunning rendition of the Star Spangled Banner, followed by a ceremonial face-off by distinguished guest Darren Pang (hockey analyst) and then the true releasing of the puck from Referee McQuiver's hand. The biggest game of my life was underway.

Sean and I, sitting side-by-side at the end of our bench, looked on through our clear helmet visors nervously at the intense battle between Avulette's Arsenault and the Trodeau Troop. Our top line got the physical play started by checking the opposing players at will. Goals would be hard to come by; Scott Hooden and Ohio State's net minder, Grand Pierre, both stepped up their games, attempting to carry the team on their shoulders to the playoffs. I could think of no one better than the Hoover to overcome that burden.

"Line three! Line three!" shouted Trodeau as the three amigos hoped over to boards to play ninety seconds of smash mouth hockey. "Hold in the neutral zone! Get on side Hutch! In the corner! Dig, dig, dig! There you go—shoot it! No! Bad call ref!" The animated coach called out orders incessantly from his stationery pedestal behind the row of Michigan players. While digging the puck out of a corner, Trodeau's baritone voice rung through my ears as if he was standing beside me. Now imagine being seated on the bench directly in front of the coach.

Freshman Marc DeShriver came down with an injury at the nine-minute mark from a vicious (and illegal) clip to his thigh. Gerry and myself slowly helped the defenseman off the ice, favoring one leg, as the crowd applauded his toughness. This was the type of game Ohio State played—nasty and hard-hitting. Coach Trodeau begged for patience and instead of retaliating, we responded by netting a goal; Eric Lessard's third of the tournament, assisted by Perner and Kotti. The wound on the scoreboard hit them harder than a retribution fight would have.

Second period. Ohio State erased our lead only forty seconds into the middle frame by a breakaway backhanded shot that slid between Scott's legs. This momentarily took the wind out of our sails. In turn, the Buckeyes notched another score only minutes later to give them a 2-1 advantage. I wasn't on the ice for either goal but our once-energetic line certainly didn't help the team in the second twenty. We recorded merely two shots on Grand Pierre and spent the majority of our three shifts in our own zone, unable to clear the puck out of harm's way. Given the circumstances, we were damn lucky to keep the biscuit out of the basket.

Third period. Marc DeShriver valiantly returned to the bench after receiving a painful cortisone shot from Trainer Blackwell. Every one of our players tapped the rookie and said something like 'go get 'em buddy'. Cortisone shots are no small thing. It's been proven that they have slowly ruined the careers of more than a handful of NHL greats.

The time to shine was upon us. Twenty minutes was all that remained on the scoreboard for us to tie up this game—or else the season would be over. Walsh, the team's vocal captain, pulled us together before the period commenced to share his thoughts. We all gathered in a cluster and listened to him say:

"This is it boys. We need one to tie, two to win. Let's group together and get this thing done! The time is now! 'Win' on three...one, two, three—"

"Win!"

The colorful blue and yellow sections rose to their feet; students, parents and supporters alike playing the sixth man. I don't believe they sat until they reached their cars. Ohio State's crowd matched our applause, making the stadium rumble as the puck was dropped. "College hockey at its finest," the newspapers would soon report; believe me, the columnists would have a field day with *this* game.

Lessard took the face-off and played alongside Perner and winger Nolan Van Eaves for one hundred and twenty seconds of an incredible fast pace. My eyes barely kept up with the rapid puck movement. "Bring it up! Out to your wing Eric! Throw it at the net!"

Eighteen minutes remained when the second line got their chance. Jeff Thomas and Strick played a two-man game (practiced repeatedly during the week) and came incredibly close to scoring the equalizer on a hard wrist shot. Grand Pierre dove to his weak side, making the nifty glove save. "Awww!" the Michigan crowd groaned. "Hooray!" shouted the Buckeyes.

Fifteen minutes—my turn. I bombarded onto Detroit's ice with my usual mates and the top defensive pairing. One shot, no luck. I had wound up from the blue line and sent the puck directly into the net minder's chest. "Hooray!" "Awww!"

Eleven minutes. We successfully killed off a two-minute minor penalty, only allowing two opposing scoring chances. The momentum began to swing in our favor.

Nine minutes. The score was stuck at 2-1 as time was rapidly running thin. Coach Trodeau ordered my third line out for another final period shift. Butterflies hatched in the pit of my stomach and flapped around my insides, fully realizing the severity of this moment. "Get on the puck! Set up the number five offense! Four forwards wide! Come on boys, we need a score!" I used every ounce of adrenaline left (and even pushed myself past the limit) but couldn't find a way to break the goal's seal. Following those trying two minutes, I came to the bench winded and prayed for better luck from the second unit. There would be none.

Three minutes left. I expected to ride the bench for the remainder of the game; Trodeau would use Lessard's line with Gerry and Tom for the duration. I was regulated to the crappy role of cheerleader.

"Let's go guys, put one in!" All sixteen thousands hearts had risen to their throats.

"Let's go Janni, turn it up," cheered a tired and sweaty Sean, watching his teammate fly up the right wing boards and into the opponent's zone. "He has Eric with him—in front! Put it in front Janni!" Eric Lessard, who had vanquished his defensemen at the red line, streaked up the middle creating a 2-on-1 opportunity. "Eric's open!" The Frenchman saw a deep blue jersey with blonde trim out of the corner of his eye and slapped a passed around the trailing Ohio State player, straight on to Lessard's stick. Without hesitation, he wrapped a shot from six feet. The black blurred puck sailed at Grand Pierre and then was lost in his pads. The crowd grew quiet.

Two minutes. The entire bench for both teams leaned over the boards to search for the missing puck. Grand Pierre lay in the crease, legs split out to either side, also participating in the hunt. He spun his head and neck 180 degrees, only to watch the puck slowly glide through the crease and cross the plane of the goal. From dead silence, a deafening cheer filled the arena; Michigan fans leaping in the air and Buckeye followers collapsing to the floor. As for us, we went ballistic. Hugs were plentiful and humongous grins couldn't be concealed, but the famed coach remained steady and calm. The championship game was tied at two.

"University of Michigan goal scored by number nine, Eric Lessard, assisted by number seventeen Janni Perner and number five, Gerry Walsh. Time of the goal is eighteen minutes and eleven seconds. Lessard by Perner and Walsh at eighteen eleven of the third."

Play continued and the game remained tied until Trodeau wisely called our single timeout at the nineteen forty-eight mark. Twelve seconds sat like a ticking time bomb on the scoreboard.

"Let's gather around boys," called our unbelievably tranquil leader. The clipboard was thrust between us, cluttered with black markings (soon to be explained). We huddled tight as the opening to *Eye Of The Tiger* pounded loudly from the hanging speakers. Dut...dut dut dut...dut dut dut...dut dut daaaaa! This scene took me back five years where the exact song played at the championship match between Michigan and Ferris State. My father and I sat in the upper balcony's first row of the Joe Louis Arena along with our fellow Dekers from the Blue Line Club. The game was much like this one; very defensive and physical, forcing both squads to expend all their channeled energy. Exhausted beyond belief, forward Josh Langfeld somehow wove a pass into Comrie who amazingly wailed the puck into the back of the net. Michigan went on to win the CCHA championship by a score of 2-1 that evening, making it their third consecutive title. Dad and I remained for the post-game awards, which the memory really centered on. It was one of those moments that never fade from one's mind. Each member of the big blue roster were announced by the division president and allowed to individually hoist the trophy high above their heads. Most fought tears. After the ceremony concluded, all twenty skaters made a victory lap around the ice, each passing the championship cup to one another. What an amazing moment. It wasn't even something I could prepare for—it just happens.

"Alright, here's the play," said our focused coach pointing to his masterpiece. He circled his head to meet everybody's staring eyes. Not a single one of us did so much as blink and a pin dropping could be heard between our bodies. The team had come together. "Lessard, Thomas, Janni, Callie, Walsh and Kotti, I want you six all out there. There's only twelve seconds left so we're going to roll the dice and pull the goalie." Jerry Trodeau took a quick second for us to comprehend his strategy and then said in the steadiest of voices; "Boys...we're going for the win."

Author's Note

I was nineteen years old when I got the inspiration to write the *Dekers Blue Line Club***.** I immediately began to formulate ideas and during my final semester at the University Of Massachusetts-Amherst, when I was twenty, I began to write every evening as an escape from the depression of college. This is not to say college is indeed depressing, but I was stuck at a dead end out in Amherst and already knew a transfer of schools was in store for me. Often, I would write in the evening when the lights went out in our dormitory room (which in reality was the basement of a dormitory). While my two roommates snored the night away, I would swivel my desk lamp over my bed and get lost in the fresh novel.

Upon transferring to the new college, I took a three-month break from writing completely. Instead, I opted to focus on my new major (business administration) and solely concentrate on schoolwork. It was April of 2002 when I resumed the story-turned-novel, writing during breaks between classes, nights with no homework, weekends at friend's houses; basically every chance I got.

Finally, at the ripe old age of twenty-one, my first novel was complete. It took considerable time to piece everything together and finish it exactly how I wanted, but the gratification I felt on that one cold March evening is indescribable.

Writing a novel is a trying, however, enjoyable experience. Over the total fifteen months from start to finish, writing carried me from the real world to the fantasy that lay within the *Dekers Blue Line Club.*